THIS HOUSE

SIAN NORTHEY
THIS HOUSE

Translated from the Welsh
by Susan Walton

3TimesRebel

First published by 3TimesRebel Press in 2024, our third year of existence.

Title: *This House* by Sian Northey

Original title: *Yn y Tŷ Hwn*
Copyright © Sian Northey, 2011
English translation rights arranged with
Y Lolfa Cyf.
Talybont, Ceredigion SY24 5AP
Cymru/Wales, UK
ylolfa@ylolfa.com
www.ylolfa.com

Originally published by Gomer Press.

Translation from the Welsh: Copyright © Susan Walton, 2024

Design and layout: Enric Jardí

Illustrations: Anna Pont Armengol

Editing and proof reading: Greg Mulhern, Bibiana Mas

Maria-Mercè Marçal's poem *Deriva*:
© heiresses of Maria-Mercè Marçal

Translation of Maria-Mercè Marçal's poem *Deriva*:
© Dr Sam Abrams

This translation was done with the support of the Literature Wales Mentoring Scheme, a partnership project with the National Centre for Writing, funded by Arts Council England, and Wales Literature Exchange, funded by The National Lottery through the Arts Council of Wales.

With special thanks to Wales Literature Exchange for their financial support.

Cyfnewidfa Lên Cymru
Wales Literature Exchange

Printed and bound by CMP Digital Print Solutions,
Poole, Dorset, England
Paperback ISBN: 978-1-7391287-9-1
eBook ISBN: 978-1-7394528-2-7 / 978-1-7394528-3-4

www.3timesrebel.com

Sian Northey and Susan Walton have asserted their moral rights to be identified respectively as the Author and the Translator of this work.

All rights reserved. Reprinting, online posting or adaptation of the whole or any part of this work without the prior written permission of the Publisher is prohibited except for short quotations as allowed by law in fair use in such as a review.

A CIP catalogue record for this book is available from the British Library.

*For Twm
and to the memory of Iwan
S.N.*

*This translation is for Bronwen.
It is also dedicated to Gwenlli, for patiently and
constructively listening to all my translations, and to the
memory of Dafydd, who didn't get to read it.
S.W.*

1

IT HAD TAKEN ANNA HALF AN HOUR TO CARRY THE LOGS INTO the house and the fire in the wood burner was almost out. Leaning one of her crutches against the wall, she dropped the rucksack from her back. She emptied the wood out, putting the smallest, driest pieces straight onto the fire and piling the rest in a tidy stack at the side of the stove. She turned suddenly, and stuck two fingers up at the mob staring at her through the window, then laughed out loud.

'Blimey, if there really was someone out there, they'd think I'd lost my marbles. An old woman going totally gaga. And talking to herself.'

Maybe it would be nice to have a cat again. There had been no pets in Nant yr Aur for a good few years now, but a kitten would be fun. After this leg mends, she thought, maybe I'll look for a kitten and it'll grow into a big moggy – one that can purr – and then it'll die and be buried under the hedge with the rest.

She turned back to face the window and raised her middle finger this time, before giving the fire a poke, reaching for her crutch and moving to the chair.

'Five minutes' sit-down, before fetching more.'

She felt pleased her plan had worked. She could cope, there was no need for her to quit because of some silly little accident. Nor because of her age. Though scared of falling again and damaging her ankle, she was sure she'd made the right decision in refusing to talk things through with the social services woman before leaving hospital. She didn't need anybody. She looked once more at the logs. Maybe this wasn't the best fate for an expensive Karrimor rucksack, but she wasn't likely to use it ever again for anything more adventurous. She managed to make the trip three times, carefully avoiding the remaining snow that clung to the slate slabs in front of the door. Then she'd had enough.

One last thing before sitting down, she thought. She went through to the back to fetch some scissors, cut the plastic bracelet off her wrist, and threw it on the fire. She watched as it half-melted, half-burned and felt a shiver go through her. She sank into the chair and watched the flames, feeling the house relax around her. She could sense the rooms snuggling up together like little piglets in straw. She knew she should cook something, or at least make herself a cheese sandwich. She'd eaten nothing at lunchtime, and only a small piece of toast for breakfast. But by now the sheer stubborn energy that had allowed her to carry the firewood in had disappeared. The kitchen felt far, far away; the whisky bottle was close at hand. She poured a generous inch into the glass that was still on the side table since the other night. Whisky was a new habit. She'd always been a gin woman. But a few months back, in the middle of her monthly shopping expedition to the supermarket, she was drawn – almost inexplicably – to a bottle of expensive single malt. She'd justified the decision by reasoning that she'd probably drink less of something she didn't particularly like.

But before long she'd developed a taste for this golden liquid. Not that she got stupidly drunk on her own. No, the days of getting stupidly drunk were long gone. The nights of dancing on tables and crying because whales were becoming extinct. No, those days were long gone. But she had seen the look on the paramedic's face as he'd caught a whiff of whisky on her breath.

Never mind. She was glad of the comfort of the Glenmorangie tonight, and glad too of the quiet comfort of the house: a contrast to the hurly-burly of the hospital. When the phone rang, for a moment she was tempted to ignore it. If it had been on the other side of the room, she would have; but it was on the side table, beside the bottle of whisky. She recognised neither the voice nor the name. A man, possibly middle-aged, maybe younger – certainly a good deal younger than Anna – enquiring if she'd received the letter he'd sent her.

'I've been ...' For some reason Anna hesitated. 'I've been away. I only got home today, and I haven't looked at my post yet.'

A log shifted in the grate and Anna heard herself promise that she would consider his offer and answer him. She assured him there would be a prompt reply in the post and that there was no need for him to phone again. As she placed the phone back on the table she realised he hadn't said what the offer was, and that she hadn't asked.

She left the whisky half-finished and hobbled into the kitchen. It was colder in there. She put two handfuls of tagliatelle on to boil, and took a jar of pesto out of the fridge. Cheating cooking. The letters were waiting for her in a pile on the kitchen table. While the pasta was boiling she started going through them – two get-well-soon cards, an electricity bill, junk mail that could go straight onto the fire, and a white envelope with her name misspelled on it. She opened the envelope and started to read, letting the pasta overcook. She rescued it before it turned completely mushy, spooned some pesto over it and took the bowl into the living room to eat her meal in front of the fire. The letter was already folded and stuffed into the back pocket of her jeans; there was no need for her to look at it again.

'No,' was the answer, of course. Had she wished to sell, she would have done so years ago. She had received far better offers; good money that would have enabled her to start a new, totally different, life. But there was an understanding, a covenant of sorts. She'd understood that the day she'd first stepped over the threshold of Nant yr Aur. Or maybe she was imagining that now – that day was so long ago, as distant as yesterday.

Of course, even before that day she had been here, years before that day. But only outside the house. Being primed, perhaps, while she was still only a child. The first time she saw Nant yr Aur she was alone, a child of eleven, rather lonely, slightly romantic, wandering on her own with her dog. She had a clear image in her head of Meg, the red Welsh collie, running through the rushes down to the river. In those days Anna roamed by herself from morning until teatime without anyone worrying about her, because she was lucky enough to have been born in a time and place where such things as paedophiles didn't exist. Or, at least, no one was prepared to admit they existed.

And she saw the empty house, in a desolate spot, far from anywhere. She sat beside the door to eat her cheese sandwich, feeling as if she were the owner. She kept quiet about the place at first, in case mentioning it amidst the shouting and bickering would soil Nant yr Aur. But even when she told her parents about the house beside the river, in the cwm with mountains all around and a raven flying above, she was met with such an offhand response she might as well have kept it secret. And before long, she couldn't remember whether she'd told her parents or not.

Even in her teens, she would wander there when things were bad at home: when there was a bruise on her mother's cheek, and her father was scarcely bothering to hide the bottles in the airing cupboard. By now Meg was too old to come with her, and instead of eating a cheese sandwich Anna would enjoy a quiet cigarette, sitting on the doorstep and letting the house comfort her. She never saw anyone else there. Maybe that was why it was so easy to believe she owned Nant yr Aur. She never knocked on the door, just put her thumb on the latch each time, in case it was unlocked and she could go in and pretend that this was her home. The door was always locked, and home was still where she and her mother walked on eggshells, the place where the neighbours paid no heed to the shouting.

But by the time she first entered Nant yr Aur her mother was dead and her befuddled father was in a care home.

Goodness knows exactly why she headed there that day. A postponed meeting had freed her up for the whole afternoon, the weather was gorgeous, a song from her childhood had been on the radio and then circling in her head all morning. Maybe that was why. She liked to think it was fate, a coincidence engineered by someone or by something.

Whatever the reason, she drove to her childhood home, parked there and started to walk: the rough track running alongside the lake, then a path leading through the gap between two small hills. Up she climbed, somewhat out of breath, to the flat rock, and then she looked down, half-afraid. Afraid it wouldn't be there, afraid it would be a ruin, or that some bugger would have tastelessly 'done it up' and stuck a conservatory on the front, or that the Forestry Commission would have planted up the surrounding land. But no, from this distance at least, it looked exactly as it had a quarter of a century earlier: seeming to grow out of the rock, the stream running in front of it. Perhaps the fields were more overgrown with rushes, but to all intents and purposes it was the same. She looked down at her legs, expecting to see the bare, brown legs of an eleven-year-old, and gazed in surprise at the thighs of a woman in her thirties. She almost called for Meg to follow her on the last stretch down the slope and along the flat ground to the house.

The doorway of Nant yr Aur was wide, with stones laid edgewise to form an archway. When she was a child, the door was made from oak planks – without decoration, without paint or varnish – and it was still the same now. She walked straight up to it and, out of force of habit, put her thumb on the latch and pushed. And for the first time ever, the door opened. It swung open easily, all the way, wide open. There was no time to falter, to think twice. The room was decorated very simply, with a roaring wood fire in the large fireplace at the far end, the inglenook stacked high with logs. But it was a room without a living soul. She stepped inside. There was a bowl of fruit on the circular oak table, and without thinking she took up a handful of grapes and ate them unhurriedly, one by one, while looking slowly and contemplatively around the room.

'"*And who's been eating my fruit?*" said Daddy Bear,' thundered a voice from somewhere above her head.

She dropped the grapes that were still in her hand, and by the time she'd turned towards the voice she was thirty-four years old again.

On the open landing at the far end of the room stood a man who was obviously in the middle of dressing – jeans, feet bare, his shirt in his hand, and his hair wet.

'I'm sorry, I don't normally ... You must think that ...'

Mid-stammer, she noticed that the eyes above her were sparkling and the mouth was trying hard not to laugh at her.

'Take a seat, I'll be down in two minutes to tell you what I think.'

Anna looked towards the open door. If she'd had a car outside, she'd have bolted. But the thought of trying to outrun him over the moorland and up onto the higher slopes, or down the rough track through the valley in the direction of the sea stopped her. Or maybe she craved a longer stay in Nant yr Aur.

She sat down in one of the armchairs in front of the fire – in almost exactly the spot where she sat now – and waited.

She did not have to wait long. The man, tall and still barefoot, came down the steep wooden stairs, but with his shirt on now and carrying a towel to dry his hair. As he passed the front door, he gave it a shove to close it.

'To keep the heat in.'

The door was solid, and she knew it was the only one. At least this stranger was Welsh, or at least spoke Welsh. She had that same innocent faith in the goodness of other Welsh people, of the 'we', shared by middle-class parents who would allow little Ffion, who normally wouldn't be permitted to walk home from school unaccompanied, to roam freely around the National Eisteddfod field for hours.

'Cup of tea?'

'Um ... thanks. No milk or sugar.'

'Lemon? Earl Grey? Darjeeling?'

He disappeared through the door opposite her, and Anna remained sitting in stunned surprise. The last thing she'd expected that morning was a cup of Earl Grey tea in Nant yr Aur.

From the direction of the kitchen she could hear the sound of crockery, but neither of them made any attempt at conversation between the two rooms. Anna looked around. She made a conscious effort to try and remember it all, in case she was never given the chance to be within the walls of Nant yr Aur again. It was obviously a holiday home – there were none of the bits and pieces one would find in a normal home, even the tidiest one – and yet she could see that he'd been there a while. The corner by the window had been made into a makeshift office – a desk, computer, paperwork and books. She'd have to get up from her chair to take a peek at the books: dictionaries were the only ones she could make out at a distance. Well, she'd already stolen the grapes, so she might as well be hanged for a sheep as for a lamb.

She was looking at a picture on the wall when he came back into the room carrying two china mugs of tea and a chocolate cake; she hadn't made it as far as the desk. He handed her the tea, and went to sit in front of the fire, obviously expecting her to follow suit.

'Ioan, Ioan Gwilym,' he said, smiling that smile again.

'Anna Morris. Look, I'm sorry, the door has never been open before ... I didn't know there was anyone here ... I've been wanting ...'

The cheeky so-and-so was laughing at her again. Anna reached for a piece of cake to hide her confusion, and took a bite.

'This is good. Did you make it yourself, Mr Gwilym?'

Stupid question. Would a man – an academic, an author, whatever he was – in the middle of nowhere spend his time baking chocolate cakes on the off-chance that someone would call by for tea? She'd best make her excuses as soon as possible, she thought, before she said or did anything else stupid.

'Ioan,' he said, 'if you're going to walk into my house and help yourself to fruit, we'd better be on first-name terms; and, yes, I made the cake.'

Looking back, perhaps that was the moment Anna fell in love with him.

'It's pretty good, Ioan.'

***

Tonight, Anna could remember the taste of the cake and how the room was furnished that day more easily than she could recall Ioan's face. She tried to recreate his face, to imagine him sitting in the chair opposite her, but it refused to appear.

But suddenly, for a second, she heard his voice from the back kitchen, 'You're as stubborn as a mule, Anna.'

'Mules are wise beasts,' she said, topping up her whisky.

'And terribly attractive too,' said the voice.

2

ANNA LOWERED HERSELF ONTO THE BED WITH A SIGH. STAIRS and crutches were not a good combination, but she was determined to sleep in her own room rather than on the sofa downstairs. As she tugged at her jeans, the letter fell out of the pocket. She tossed her clothes onto a chair in an untidy heap and retrieved the letter, putting it on the bedside table. Once she was comfortable, with the hot water bottle in its knitted cover lying next to her free leg, she picked the letter up once more and re-read it.

At some point she would have to take such things seriously. Not now, but at some point. She would answer this man tomorrow. There was no reason not to be courteous. And he'd sounded pleasant enough on the phone. The days of being able to picture someone from their handwriting were long gone, and all she had to go on was the address on the envelope and the signature. And the style in which the letter was written, of course, though there was nothing exceptional about that – unless you count grammatically correct Welsh as exceptional, snapped the irritable old woman who sometimes inhabited her body.

That body had changed so much since the day Ioan asked her to come and live with him. She had hesitated for a moment, and he'd tried again.

'Come and live at Nant yr Aur.'

And she came, and she stayed. But unless she made a conscious effort to remind herself of the bare facts, she often felt it was Ioan who had come to live with her at Nant yr Aur.

She put the letter back in its envelope, switched off the light and lay there looking through the skylight at the stars. Ever since primary school, when she'd first understood that looking at stars was to look at something that no longer necessarily existed, she had delighted in this fact. The light from them keeps on coming, keeps coming, keeps coming across all those miles, but by the time it reaches earth, by the time it reached her eyes, the star itself has disappeared, has died, has ceased to exist.

Like every pair of lovers, she and Ioan had gazed at the stars. In the winter they had lain in this bed and stared at them, but in the summer they would drag a blanket outside and lie on the bank of the stream, hand in hand. How many stars had died since then, their light still reaching Nant yr Aur? But of course – and she smiled at the thought – by now there were new stars in existence, and their light had yet to reach Nant yr Aur. Some of these were stars that hadn't existed at all when she was holding Ioan's hand; others had existed then, but their light still hadn't arrived. And there were likely some that she could see today, their light unseen back then, even though they had been there. The thing was so miraculously complicated and massive. Massive beyond any comprehension. Her brain struggled to recall a line of poetry: something about pools in a stream that 'scarce could bathe a star'.

'It's not his best work, you know,' said Ioan's voice.

Anna ignored his voice for a moment to pin down the verse once more.

> Where the wandering water gushes
> From the hills above Glen-Car,
> In pools among the rushes
> That scarce could bathe a star,
> We seek for slumbering trout
> And whispering in their ears
> Give them unquiet dreams;
> Leaning softly out
> From ferns that drop their tears
> Over the young streams.
> Come away, O human child!
> To the waters and the wild
> With a faery, hand in hand,
> For the world's more full of weeping than you can understand.

And when the whole verse came back to her, the memories of that night beside the stream flooded back too.

'It's sentimental nonsense, he'd said. Where did you learn it off by heart like that?'

'In school. I like it. I always thought of here when I read it.'

She glanced at the stream and at the house behind them, and then at the man by her side. She didn't want to discuss exactly where 'here' was or what it was. Here wasn't the same thing to everyone.

'Well, our child won't be stolen by the faeries,' he said, as his fingers, which had been lying lightly and protectively on her belly, moved downwards. That was one of the advantages of a remote house, thought Anna. An advantage she could not mention to the midwives who worried about her, worried that she was often on her own while Ioan was away lecturing, worried about the difficulty of her getting to the hospital when her time came. Only one of them ventured to mention the possibility of isolation and depression following the birth. Anna had looked at her in complete disbelief. No, not quite disbelief; it wasn't that she couldn't believe her, but rather that she had no conception of such a thing. She could not conceive of herself feeling lonely or depressed at Nant yr Aur.

And she wasn't, of course – at least not then. Once their sweat had cooled, and a breeze from the sea reached them, they carried their blanket back into the house and up to their room. Ioan made them milky coffee, with a tot of whisky in each. She'd forgotten that: her liking for whisky in coffee back then. The leaflets the midwife gave her suggested avoiding alcohol, but it was unlikely that a thimbleful once a week was going to harm anyone. She knew by now that there was a long list of things that pregnant women were advised to avoid. She wouldn't have been allowed to eat soft cheese or lobster. But Ioan would bring all kinds of cheeses back from his travels, and sometimes Emyr would turn up with a lobster for her. Much as she loved the taste of lobster, she hated putting them into boiling water alive; fortunately, he was always willing to do that for her and then stay for supper. Years later she realised that Emyr had been besotted with her, but by then all sorts of things had changed.

***

'I still maintain,' said Ioan, putting his empty mug on the floor beside the bed, 'that if it's a boy, I want to call him Dylan.'

'And the poor thing will forever have to suffer English people pronouncing his name wrong.'

'That's not a good reason not to choose the name we want. Anyway, it'll be character forming for him to have to correct them.'

'Let him arrive safely first. And maybe *she'll* be Rhian.'

'Yeah, maybe she'll be Rhian,' said Ioan, suddenly sleepy.

***

Anna moved the plastered leg slowly and awkwardly, trying to relax her body as she'd relaxed on that night. Although, of course, that was never going to be possible again. That night everything and everyone, aside from the nameless being in her womb, was quiet. Ioan slept, and she lay there, conscious of the baby's movements and the exact shape of Ioan's ear. Could she recognise him from only his ear? Maybe, she decided. She would certainly recognise him from his feet; he had surprisingly wide feet for an otherwise slim man: with a high instep and the big toe like ... Yes, she would recognise his feet. Then she started to think about his socks, idly considering what he would need to take with him on his trip to Paris the day after tomorrow. This wasn't to be a long trip, and he'd be home long before the baby was due.

She'd declined the offer to go with him. She almost always declined, in any case. She had a genuine reason every time. She once tried to explain that what she wanted to avoid was coming back to Nant yr Aur with Ioan and, as they approached home, imagining the house empty, without either of them there. She knew she hadn't explained it properly.

As she packed his case the next day she tucked little notes – loving but silly messages – into the folds of some of his clothes. She put a smooth pebble from the river into the pocket of his suit jacket. She knew that he put his hands in his pockets as he lectured.

The final month of her pregnancy, after Ioan had returned from that trip to Paris, was a part of her life that seemed to have been held in a frame. There was nothing within the frame except a perfect, completely perfect, square of the most ravishing colour in existence. And sometimes, even today, she was able to slip back into that square. Perhaps only for a moment, but it still existed somewhere.

And then, suddenly, there were all sorts of colours in the frame. Dylan was born.

3

THERE WAS A KNOCK AT THE DOOR AND AN UNCEREMONIOUS 'Anyone home?' early the next morning, before Anna had even boiled the kettle.

'Two sacks of coal. Right by the door for you. You should have warned me you were coming home yesterday.'

'Cuppa?'

'Best not. Dora's expecting me back.'

Anna looked at him through the window, walking back towards his Land Rover. Emyr is ageing, she thought. Seventy years old and able to carry a sack of coal with no bother, but he was ageing. She went to the door and looked at the two sacks, smiling when she saw the packet of firelighters perched on one of them. The difference between 'users of firelighters' and 'collectors of kindling' was an old, old in-joke between them. Its origins were lost in the mists of time, but the gist of the joke was that 'kindling people' are full of mischief and 'firelighter types' are boring. And now here they both were: firelighter types.

'Not for long,' she said, carrying the packet into the house. 'Not for long.'

Their unfamiliar smell clung to her fingers, and every small task took far, far longer than usual. She persevered until the coal had caught, a little of the wood she'd brought in yesterday lay on top of it, the room was warm, she'd spread butter and marmalade on her toast, and the coffee was brewing in the red coffee pot that Ioan had brought back from Paris before Dylan was born. The red enamel was a maze of tiny cracks, but otherwise it was in good shape, considering it had been used daily for almost thirty years. She wrote the letter as she finished her second cup. The words did not need much thought.

Dear Mr Williams,
Thank you for your letter and for your offer, which seems fair – indeed generous. Unfortunately, I do not intend selling Nant yr Aur

She considered explaining further. She swallowed a mouthful of coffee. She placed a neat full stop at the end of the letter.

Yours sincerely,
Anna Morris

She looked at her signature. This had been her name her whole life: certain, sure. She remembered the discussion there had been about Dylan's second name. She'd given in on that too, telling herself that it didn't really matter.

'Everyone will call him Dylan Nant yr Aur anyway, you'll see.'

'Not if ...'

Ioan had left the sentence unfinished. This battle was one he'd won.

Not that they really fought. They never had rows. Turning the other cheek, giving way, avoiding confrontation ... that was Anna's nature. She hadn't been born like that, but that was her nature by the end of her childhood. Shortly after she and Ioan met, well before there was any thought of Dylan, even before Anna had moved into Nant yr Aur, they'd gone out for a meal at a local pub. They'd both been dithering, unable to decide at which table to sit, when he'd asked, 'Will you ever tell me what to do?'

'No, probably not.'

He'd looked at her in amazement.

'If it's something important, I'll decide what I'm going to do. If you're lucky, I'll let you know,' she'd told him.

They'd sat down at the nearest table, ordered food, and it was Ioan who had chosen the wine.

***

That was a long time ago. Anna placed the letter to Siôn Williams in an envelope, sealed it, and put a stamp on it. One of the envelopes from her get-well-soon cards lay on the table: thick paper of a horrible pale puce colour. She started writing on it, like a child, filling every part: Anna Morris, Nant yr Aur; Anna Morris, Nant yr Aur; Anna Morris, Nant yr Aur ... Changing the handwriting, sometimes curved and neat, the next a scrawl, but keeping the wording the same. Exactly the same.

She had written those same words over and over the summer Dylan was ill. It is astonishing how much paperwork sickness involves, how many times it has to be confirmed that you are you, and that you are the mother of Dylan Gwilym, and that Ioan Gwilym is the father of Dylan Gwilym, and this is the correct phone number, and that you all live together in Nant yr Aur. Submitting the details tidily on dotted lines, or confining them within rectangular boxes, and then reading them again on the ugly strip of plastic wrapped around his small wrist.

Before that summer, the three of them had cut themselves off from the world, playing house for almost two years. She had given up work, Ioan was earning a good salary and was generous, totally happy to be the breadwinner. Later on, she sometimes wondered about this, but at least that was how things appeared at the time. In Dylan's waking hours, her world revolved around him. Nothing was more important than 'This little piggy went to market, this little piggy stayed home ...' And when Dylan slept she would be busy painting the kitchen bright yellow and making curtains for the little bedroom and planting beans. And when Ioan was home, she loved him in the gaps between reciting nursery rhymes and putting up shelves.

But then, suddenly, there was no time to weed the beans or wash the windows or strip paint from wood that had been painted and paint wood that had been bare.

Ioan suggested, one starless night when there was no point in looking through the skylight, that they should move because they had so far to drive to the hospital.

'Not a long-term thing. Rent somewhere closer to ... So you have less travelling to do. There are nice little places to rent. Somewhere with a garden, of course ...'

'No.'

Anna got up to go and look at Dylan in the little bedroom. And then she went downstairs, confidently guiding herself along in the dark, her hands caressing the walls as she passed. She returned, carrying two mugs of tea, and she and Ioan drank without a word and then made love tenderly and deliberately. And Anna cried after she'd come, big snotty tears, but Ioan didn't ask what it was about – merely held her and reached for his shirt, which was on the floor beside the bed, to dry her face with it and then let her use it to blow her nose on. It was good quality cotton, and hardly dirty at all – a pale blue with the narrowest of darker blue stripes, with only the faintest smell of sweat.

And then Ioan went to London for a week, and when he came home there was no making love. Anna was in the hospital with Dylan, sleeping on a chair at his bedside. Months later she realised that she'd never asked Ioan where he was sleeping when he left the hospital at night, but he must have been staying somewhere nearby. When all three of them arrived back at Nant yr Aur after a few days, the house was exactly as she'd left it. And while Dylan was playing with his old toys and ignoring the expensive new plastic ones they'd bought on the way home, it was almost possible to believe that the previous four days had never happened. Ioan set about making food, and cut his finger slicing meat. When he went back into the living room to ask her if there were any sticking plasters in the house, Anna was sound asleep in the chair near the window.

She woke up two hours later –with a blanket over her, Dylan in bed, a roaring fire in the grate and Ioan sitting reading. Without moving, Anna looked carefully around the room. It was difficult to believe that every window and every piece of furniture and every door were at exactly the same angles as they had been a week ago.

4

EMYR REAPPEARED SOMETIME MID-AFTERNOON. MILK, A LOAF, cheese, three tomatoes. He plonked them down on the table.

'I'll have that tea now,' he said. Anna reached for the crutches.

'Sit down, woman. I'll make it.'

And the pair of them sat quietly at the kitchen table, watching the rain that was busy washing away what remained of the snow.

'How much do I owe you for these?'

'You can pay me another time. I'll put them on the bill.'

'How long's that piece of paper by now, Emyr?'

'It's like a bloody toilet roll. You'll have to sell this shack to afford to pay me back.'

Emyr was probably the only person in the world who could say that and receive nothing but a smile from Anna.

'Speaking of which, can you post this for me on your way home?'

As he pushed the letter into his pocket he caught sight of the name on the envelope. He was thankful that Anna was stowing the cheese and milk in the fridge, her back to him. And yet it was a common enough name – there must be dozens, if not hundreds, of men called Siôn Williams in the world.

But as he left, Emyr kissed her lightly on her cheek, something he had not done for a long time.

'Almost forgot. Dora is asking if you'd like to come for supper one night.'

'Thank you, but ...'

'Well, I've asked, haven't I?'

And they smiled at each other.

Anna stood at the door watching him walk towards the Land Rover. 'Emyr,' she shouted, 'thanks for the firelighters.'

He didn't even turn his head, merely waved an acknowledgement. And she remained by the door, watching the Land Rover disappear.

She couldn't see him stop beside the postbox set into the wall at the edge of the village, but she was sure he would. She could depend on Emyr. And of course Emyr stopped to post the letter, although he did look for a long time at the name and address on the envelope before pushing it through the slot into the darkness.

Anna didn't think Emyr had driven anything except a blue Land Rover for decades. A succession of them, as if they were breeding, the old ones left to rust in the corner of a field. Or at least that was how it had been when he was at Ty'n Giât.

The latest vehicle was the only one that got to park outside the neat little bungalow in the village where he and Dora now spent their evenings sitting in front of their gas fire. Like the others, this latest Land Rover was bound to end its days at

Ty'n Giât, where the lads would set it in its final resting place and use it as an occasional kennel.

The blue Land Rover was often to be seen at Nant yr Aur the summer Dylan was poorly. Emyr had become something of a stranger since the arrival of children, but then he had started calling again. Still, the times he called during those months were almost always when Ioan was home.

'I'm going fishing with Emyr,' Ioan would proclaim.

'We're going for a pint, me and Emyr.'

'Emyr's asked me to help him move the shearlings.'

Anna suspected that Ioan didn't have a clue what a shearling was. But getting out of the house was bound to be a relief for Ioan, far away from the shelf of medicines in the kitchen, and the child growing thinner with every passing day, and the wife who hadn't had time to wash her own hair.

She saw Dora in town one afternoon that summer. Dylan was back in hospital, but he'd managed to sleep for a while and the nurses had persuaded her to go out for once. She'd refused until one of them – she'd forgotten their names by now, but it was the one with short red hair – had asked if she wouldn't mind buying some mascara for her if she was going down into town, to save her having to go at the end of her shift. She'd written down the details on a scrap of paper, and explained which shop. That was the only thing Anna had intended to do – she couldn't be bothered doing anything else.

But she happened to see Dora. Dora had left her daughter, who was two months younger than Dylan, with her mother, and had obviously been making the most of her chance to shop and was on her way to a cafe before heading home.

'Come on, it'll do you good.'

And Anna followed her meekly, looking at Dora's red shoes and wondering how anyone could spend a whole day going round the shops in such creations.

'Emyr's coming over to yours a lot these days, isn't he. Send him home if he's being a nuisance and getting under your feet, what with the little one being so ill.'

'Yes, he's calling. But I don't see much of him. He and Ioan disappear ...'

Anna looked at the sugar bowl on the table and considered adding some to her coffee, although she never usually did. She scooped the tiniest amount onto the tip of her spoon, letting it fall into the mud-coloured liquid and stirring for longer than necessary.

'Men! They're all the same, every single one. Clever men like your Ioan, and the ones like Emyr.'

Dora saw the look on Anna's face and corrected herself.

'Not that Emyr's thick. He reads a lot, but he didn't go to college, did he. They're all the same, every single one, under your feet but never around when you want them.'

And then, almost as a child would, she completely changed the course of the conversation and started a good-natured monologue about every scandal and half-scandal and possible scandal in the village and valley. Anna hardly said a word; she felt she could have stood on her head on the yellow plastic chair without Dora noticing, and yet when they left the cafe and parted company, Anna felt so much better.

She went to buy the mascara, and in the window of the shop next door she saw a circle of stained glass, its simple shapes creating a picture: an outline of purple mountains and an orange sunset. She went in and bought it, and as she walked thoughtfully up the hill to the hospital above the town she kept her hand in her pocket, fingering the fragile glass that had been wrapped in insufficient tissue paper. She could see it hanging in the kitchen window of Nant yr Aur, the morning sun shining through the sunset.

When Anna walked into the ward, Dylan was awake and playing quietly with a small blue car, like a kid in a film. There was a doctor sitting on the edge of his bed, looking through papers in a file. He raised his head when Anna walked in and smiled, but only with his mouth.

'Is your husband with you, Mrs Morris?'

'He's on his way home from France. He won't be here until tomorrow.' She noticed the doctor hesitate, considering, pretending to look again at the papers in the file. 'You might as well tell me now.'

She regretted saying that sentence. She regretted it the instant the doctor stood up and guided her by the elbow down the corridor towards two easy chairs. But it was too late by then, and the doctor started to read the words and figures that were on his damned papers, and offer an explanation, and offer the best evaluation he could. He offered an apology as well. She regretted her belief that she was strong enough to bear news like this on her own. In that instant, she would have given the world for one night of playing with the small blue car in ignorance. And she would have given the world to have Ioan here, holding her. But he was on a boat somewhere between Calais and England.

At some point in the night, around three in the morning, when Dylan was awake and was fed up with the blue car and every other toy and every story, Anna pulled the glass circle out of its tissue paper and showed it to him. It caught the light from the small lamp above his bed and bathed the bedcover in colour. She explained that she was going to hang it in the window just by where she washed up and he washed his plastic animals. She told him that the sunlight would shine through the glass and the coloured pattern would show on the kitchen floor.

She moved the circle so that the colours moved back and forth across his bed.

'Will it move when we go home, Mam?'

'Where do you want it to move?'

'To the table where I eat my dinner.'

Anna moved the coloured light slightly to the right across the bedcover. 'There we are. Where next?' asked Anna.

'The wonky step ... Mam and Dad's bedroom.'

'And then? Where does the light want to go next, Dylan?'

'The light wants a wee-wee ...'

'Yes?'

'The light wants to go to Dylan's bedroom.'

And that's what they were doing when Ioan walked into the ward: guiding a coloured light round Nant yr Aur. Ioan kissed her, a day's stubble rasping.

'When will we know?'

He realised his mistake immediately. She took hold of the circle of stained glass and rewrapped it in its tissue paper. She pulled the bedcover up over the little one, now lying back on the pillow holding his father's hand. Ioan turned off the lamp over the bed, and then it was time to go to the counterfeit comfort of the room at the end of the ward to drink tea and talk.

5

HAVING ONE LEG IN PLASTER AND HOPPING ABOUT THE PLACE on crutches meant basic things like hoovering and sweeping the floor were impossible, but a terrible urge to clean came over Anna a few days after coming home from hospital. She had to content herself with creating shining islands of cleanliness. She waxed the furniture using proper, old-fashioned wax. One cloth to spread, the other to buff to a shine. The evocative smell of lavender filled the house. Or, more accurately, she polished parts of the furniture, but the scent pleased her and the oak tabletop gleamed. She tried to remember the Welsh word for 'patina', the deep shine which only develops over time, a shine that reflects generations of love and use.

She hadn't opened the second leaf of the table for years. Fully extended, the table easily seated eight, but those occasions rarely arose. For years now it had been half a table, set against the wall. The day they'd bought it was a good day – it was the day after she'd agreed to come and live with Ioan, even before she'd packed up her things and left the house she had been renting at the time. The contents of a substantial lowland farm were being sold; they walked hand in hand through the mixture of buzz and sadness that is an auction. Although Ioan had set out to look for a bookcase, they left with lot number 240, a box of crockery and the table, promising themselves they'd hold dinner parties for family and friends. In the event, they invited friends over to sit round the big oak table for a meal maybe half a dozen times, and there was no family to invite except for Ioan's brother, who lived far away in Scotland.

He'd only been to Nant yr Aur twice. Once with his partner before Dylan was born, and the second time alone. Anna sometimes regretted that she'd lost touch with Huw. She had a mental picture of a rather gentle man walking up the road with his arm on his partner's shoulder, and of introducing them to Emyr.

'Huw, Ioan's brother, and John.'

And Emyr smiling and greeting them, 'How are you both?'

She explaining to Emyr that John came from a farming family in Scotland, and then in no time they were deep into a discussion about rams and suckler cows and she and Huw were completely lost.

The presents that arrived from Scotland for Dylan on his birthday and at Christmas were something else. Expensive toys that no parent would ever buy, wrapped in colourful paper with a ribbon and shiny gift bows; they were always accompanied by ridiculously large and totally tasteless cards. Anna knew the cards were still lying in one of the upstairs cupboards. All of Dylan's birthday cards were there in a box. And the sympathy cards too. They were lying on top of the birthday cards, like mould on strawberries. One day you think they're fine, and the next day you look in the fridge and they're not worth eating. And you're sorry you didn't put loads of sugar and cream on them the previous day and eat them all up, even if it made you feel sick.

There has to have been a certain point, in the middle of the night, when there is no mould on them and another point, straight afterwards, when the mould is there. But no one knows what goes on in the darkness of the fridge in the middle of the night. Not even if you tiptoe downstairs barefoot and open the door suddenly and the light flashes on.

Dylan's illness was something like that. One minute he was a kid receiving birthday cards, and the next minute condolence cards were arriving. But he wasn't receiving them, of course. It was Ioan's and Anna's names on the envelopes. She couldn't say why she'd kept them in the birthday-card box.

'Burn them,' Ioan had said.

'No, I won't. They're Dylan's.'

Even at the time she knew her reply didn't make sense. But there wasn't a great deal of sense to be had. There is no sense in the death of a three-year-old, so a touch more not making sense made no difference either way.

'I won't,' she'd said again, 'they're Dylan's, and they'll go in his box of cards.'

And there they still were to this day, smothering the birthday cards underneath.

But she did want to get rid of his clothes. Had Ioan not stopped her, she would have stuffed them unceremoniously into black bin bags the day after the funeral.

'Leave them. Not now. In case ...'

'In case what?'

'In case he sees,' he'd said, almost inaudibly.

His clothes were left for the time being and only cleared, months later, when Ioan wasn't there. She threw out every item, except for one tiny sock that had fallen behind the tank in the airing cupboard. Years later she found it, and couldn't bring herself to throw it away at any price. She placed it in her own sock drawer, and there it stayed, small and blue, with a tiger snarling at her. Or maybe smiling at her.

There had been a tiger at the zoo that she and Ioan and Dylan had visited as a new little threesome, a happy family wandering around a rundown zoo. She never forgot that tiger. It was pacing back and forth, like any caged tiger, all trace of fierceness and hope long gone. Dylan was about a year old, in a carrier on her back. The little one waved his arms, and for a second or two the tiger was transformed. It saw something small, not moving like the rest, whose weakness could be its undoing, that could be caught. A splinter of memory caught fire, a memory of doing something better than this, somewhere other than this, long ago. Despite the bars and the glass, Anna could see that Dylan would be its next meal. And then Anna saw the big cat recognise where it was: its expression and its whole body changed and it resumed its pointless pacing.

While this was going on Ioan was dawdling by the ostrich pen, and Anna tried to explain what had happened.

'It's okay, you know. It can't do anything to you or your baby.'

But she had insisted on hurrying father and son away to buy ice cream, as if that were the most pressing thing in the world, rather than explain that it wasn't for herself or Dylan that she was concerned.

Cold stuff, white and pink and full of artificial flavouring. And Dylan was tasting it for the first time in his life and pulling funny faces.

'Quick – get the camera. Take a picture!'

And all three of them had laughed, and all was right with the world once more.

***

Anna sat down on one of the dining chairs and put the lid back on the tin of wax. She was suddenly tired, and the blood in her plastered leg felt like molten lead. She regretted using up her energy to do a job that could have waited. A squirt of something and a quick wipe would have done this time. Or it could even have been left undone. A bit of dust never killed anyone. She started to make a mental list of things that could kill people, or kill them sooner than dust on furniture – a lack of food, heartbreak, earthquakes, an axe in the hands of a madman ...

'Anna,' she said aloud, 'you need to talk to people more.'

But when the phone rang on the other side of the room she remained in her chair, concentrating on folding the two cloths carefully, and placing them on top of the tin of wax. By the time she'd done that the phone had stopped ringing.

6

THAT NIGHT ANNA ATE HER SUPPER AT THE GLEAMING OAK table, rather than at the little pine table in the kitchen. She poured herself a glass of wine and lit a candle so as to enjoy the reflection of the flame in the tabletop. Over the years she'd learned – actually long before meeting Ioan – that one of the secrets to living a happy life on one's own was doing small things like this. She relearned it later on. Relearned the necessity of a bottle of wine, no matter how cheap, a bubble bath, a hardback book, and taking the phone off the hook for a couple of hours. And that living on lentil soup to afford such little luxuries was a price worth paying.

And then Ioan appeared, and in his wake came money and love and a house. An enchanted island in a sea of lentil soup. But only with hindsight did she realise it was an island.

She ate deliberately, sipped the wine, and gazed at the candle's flame, which was inclining slightly towards her in a draught from the window. She wondered if she should close the curtains. Not to prevent anyone from looking in – there was no one there. And, if there was someone, it would be someone she knew. The only reason to close the curtains was to keep the heat in and stop the draughts. She stood up and reached over to draw the two lengths of dark blue velvet together. Then she paused for a moment and stared into the darkness. For one second she thought she saw a flash of light down over the other side of the stream. And although she continued to gaze through the window for several minutes, she saw nothing more. She looked accusingly at the candle flame and the bottle of wine, as if suspecting them of playing a trick on her. She closed the curtains, put a few lumps of Emyr's coal on the fire and went back to her meal.

When she'd finished, one by one she took the dirty dishes through to the back and put them in the sink. She ran a little water over them so the food wouldn't cake on, but she couldn't be bothered to wash them. She could never do this without hearing Alexis Korner's growl in her head, singing about turning on the tap to start the water's flow, and then finding the sun. Here, in Nant yr Aur, she'd found her sun. She'd come back here after going to the big city. And she wasn't away long. That had been a long-ago itch, the urge to do something rather than nothing, a hope that the busyness would fill the emptiness. But home she came after a few months. Here, on her own, was the only place she could grieve. She should have known that.

And Nant yr Aur was the only place Ioan could not come to terms with his loss.

'I can't stay here, you know that. Come with me.'

And so she came, for a while.

'I have to go home, you know that. Come with me.'

And so he came for a while. And for a year, maybe two, there had been this coming and going. And the gaps between each following the other lengthened every time. There probably had been some discussion. It was difficult to recall now. She suspected there was never a decision made, nor that either had said the words, 'You know what'd be a good plan – the one who wants to be in the flat stays in the flat, and the one who wants to stay in Nant yr Aur stays in Nant yr Aur.' She was certain that sentence was never uttered, any more than were:

'I won't see you for six months now, but I'll phone on Christmas morning.'

'No point sending another letter.'

'I'm moving, here's my new address.'

Not one of these was said. That was why Anna didn't know if the only man she'd ever loved was alive or dead. He must have been alive fifteen years ago. Anna was staying in the South of France with a friend for three months over the summer in a last-ditch attempt to shake off Nant yr Aur's hold. Despite enjoying the sun and the wine and the company, back she came. When she opened the door she could see that someone had been there. Emyr was the only one she could ask, and she'd rather ask him than leave it to someone else to tell her.

'Yes – Ioan. Didn't stay long.'

She didn't ask anything else, but as he was getting into his Land Rover Emyr turned to her.

'He looked well.'

A couple of months later, on an excruciatingly ordinary day, the postman brought a solicitor's letter informing her that she was now the owner of Nant yr Aur – she and she alone. She went to see the solicitor – a rapidly ageing young man, as befitted his dusty office – and he assured her that she hadn't inherited Nant yr Aur. The house had been transferred to her, but he couldn't reveal more than that.

'Is there a letter for me? Anything?'

The old young man shook his head, smiled, and stood up to indicate that it was time for her to leave. That night Anna read every word of the deeds, read the names of those who'd lived in Nant yr Aur before her. Sitting in front of the fire, she read through them two or three times, resisting some mad urge to let each page fly up the chimney like letters to Santa. Not long afterwards she bought a wood burner. Every so often during those first few years, she would read over every word of the deeds, from the beginning to the signature of Anna Morris on the last page of the heavy paper. She hadn't looked at them for years now, and was only occasionally conscious of the succession of signatures that proved something – though what, she couldn't say.

Emyr was the only one who knew about the inexplicable appearance of the deeds. Everyone else could think what they wished. She remembered Dora asking her if the house would have to be sold, and Anna answering with no more than a shrug. Sometimes even Dora realised she'd gone too far.

But she did discuss the matter with Emyr. Or maybe Emyr just listened. Talking with Emyr tended to be like that. But this was how Emyr knew that she could sell if she really needed money to buy tomatoes and firelighters.

Anna smiled now as she thought about the firelighters. She rose and put another log on the fire, then moved clumsily to the door and pushed the bolt home. It was stiff from lack of use, and its unfamiliar squeal brought a wave of comfort.

7

ANNA WAS GETTING MORE PROFICIENT AT HANDLING HER crutches now. She was able to do more, and she'd also worked out what was impossible. It was similar to being on holiday. She'd had to simplify her life and derive pleasure from small things. She was reading far more – and was choosing the sort of books she wouldn't normally touch. She'd happened to mention to Emyr one morning that she had nothing interesting to read. The next morning he'd appeared with half a dozen books. Looking at them, Anna was convinced he had just grabbed the first six he'd come across in his house.

Over a cup of coffee, the pair of them would discuss the way hurricanes were named and the fact that the name of a particularly destructive hurricane was never used twice. A few days later they were in the presence of Ellis Wynne, as they discussed the eighteenth-century prose of his *Gweledigaethau y Bardd Cwsg*. Anna couldn't remember the last time she and Emyr had discussed books like this, and yet they had done so many times over the years. And then they would leave the realm of the imagination and Emyr would empty out the stove's ash pan, fill her coal bucket, stack wood in a neat pile near the stove and go out to his Land Rover, deaf to her thanks.

That afternoon Anna went to sit on the bench near the door. Just sit: no book, no cuppa, no nothing. Just sitting and enjoying the sun. A raven was flying high above her head, but nothing else moved. A rambler in a red coat came into view, and Anna watched enviously as he came closer. She promised herself she'd go walking far more often, once the plaster was off and her muscles had regained their strength.

'Then I'll walk as much as I can,' she said aloud to the rambler and the raven, both too far away to hear.

She watched the rambler approach, expecting him to stick to the path that would take him past the back of the house. But, rather than do that, he followed the stream and came straight across the field towards Nant yr Aur. She expected him to apologise, and say he was lost, or to walk right past without acknowledging her as if the whole countryside was his domain. That had happened before now.

'Anna Morris?'

Anna studied the young man. For a second, she thought maybe she should recognise him.

'I'm sorry to intrude, but are you Anna Morris?'

Anna realised that she hadn't answered him the first time. 'Yes.'

'Siôn Williams.' The stranger extended his hand in a way that was a touch too formal for someone his age. 'You don't know me. Forgive me, arriving unannounced like this. But it is a beautiful afternoon and I fancied a walk. The chance to see something other than streets and houses.'

He hesitated for a moment as he realised his name hadn't rung a bell with Anna. 'It was I who wrote to you,' he said.

Anna continued to stare at him without saying a word.

'I'm aware that you've sent a reply, but I thought I'd call by in any case.'

'Would you like a cup of tea?' said Anna, reaching for her crutches.

Siôn set his heavy backpack on the ground and sat down on a chair that faced the bench. In some perverse way, Anna liked the fact that he hadn't offered to help, even though she was on crutches. He didn't even express any thanks either, just sat down to indicate that he'd accepted her offer.

Anna poured the boiling water on the leaves of Earl Grey. Some things at Nant yr Aur never changed. Earl Grey and proper leaves, not teabags, was one of these. 'Poof's tea' according to Emyr, who would dilute it with milk and kill the taste with spoonfuls of sugar, before asking for a second cup.

She couldn't begin to reckon up how many cuppas Emyr had drunk there over the years. Some slurped down in a hurry, others taken at a leisurely pace. There were periods, like now, when he'd been for a cuppa almost daily. Other times they hadn't – or she hadn't – seen him for weeks on end, months sometimes.

She'd got to know Emyr through Ioan; to start with, she had welcomed him into her world because everything and everybody to do with Ioan was brilliant. It was the same infatuation that allows many a wife to think that wearing socks with sandals is appropriate, and dubious jokes, amusing. Not that Ioan was a socks and sandals man, nor one for dubious humour. Even today, she couldn't list his failings. In one way, she never got the chance to stop being infatuated with Ioan. Sometimes she could imagine that the passion would have ended, slowly and steadily, if Dylan had lived. Maybe they would have had a row about something or other, perhaps a minor misunderstanding grown out of all proportion, and they would have separated angrily and resentfully, meanly bickering over books and crockery. But that wasn't how it was. One minute she was head over heels in love with Ioan, the next, there was some sort of gauze between them which got thicker by the day. For a while, the gauze kept her separate from every part of life and from everyone, and by the time it started to thin again, Ioan wasn't there, and she didn't know whether that was important or not.

For some reason she was thinking of Ioan as she placed mugs and sugar and a small earthenware jug of milk on the tray, while she waited for the tea to brew. After she'd done this, she realised it was impossible for her to carry the tray.

'That's what you get for letting your mind wander,' she chided herself. The thought of having to take everything off the tray and carry them out one by one was too much. She went to the door and for a moment considered the young man sitting in the sun. Sometimes, seeing boys – or, now, young men – who would be about the same age as Dylan still floored her. And for a second there was something about this one, the way he watched the stream and rubbed the back of his neck as if he'd been sitting still for too long rather than walking, awoke some memory and made her smile. Siôn turned towards her, somehow sensing that she'd been looking at him.

'You have a choice, dear,' said Anna, surprising herself with the 'dear'. 'Carry the tray out here for me, or come inside to drink your tea.'

'I'll come in, if I may.'

And Anna heard Dylan's voice, whenever they were in someone else's house, saying he 'needed a wee-wee', just so he could have a nose around upstairs.

8

ANNA LIFTED HER COPY OF THE *MABINOGI* FROM THE KITCHEN table to put it back on the shelf. She and Siôn must have discussed the story of Blodeuwedd, going back to the book to check if the flowers used to create her were named. She had been fairly sure they were, and fairly sure that yellow broom was one but then wasn't sure of the rest. That aside, it was difficult to remember what they had been talking about. She noted that they hadn't discussed his letter, despite sitting and chatting for almost two hours. Certainly, neither one of them had revealed much about their personal lives, and yet Anna felt completely at ease in his company.

She looked at the book and read the words again.

Ac yna fe gymersant hwy flodau'r deri a blodau'r banadl a blodau'r erwain ...

'Oak ... broom ... meadowsweet,' she whispered as she gently closed the book and put it back in its place on the shelf. Before she'd moved in with Ioan, her many books were kept any old how: Oriana Fallaci and Kate Roberts rubbed shoulders with Chaucer, and books would be kept in dusty heaps on tables or next to the bed for weeks, or pushed in on any shelf wherever there was space for them. But when the two libraries were merged her books had to be tamed and ordered. And although she and the books rebelled for a while, they submitted in the end.

Ioan came to take his books away bit by bit. He took them as and when he needed them. By now she was a conscientious librarian, a sinner who'd been converted from the error of her ways, keeping books neat and vertical. Sometimes she bought replacements for books he'd taken. Other times, she would just shuffle the books up to close the gaps. A few of his books remained, with his name on the title page of every one, along with the date and where it was bought.

Next to the *Mabinogi* there was an English–Latin dictionary. Anna opened it for the bittersweet pleasure of reading his handwriting inside: 'Ioan Gwilym, October 26th, 1985, in Hay with Anna'.

It had been a cold day, she recollected, cold but dry and the two of them had wandered the streets of Hay on Wye arm in arm, and then hand in hand, then like sixth-formers: each with a hand in the other's jeans pocket. It's a miracle they managed to prise themselves apart for long enough to look at any books, let alone buy one.

Although there were some book shops there, Hay was far less touristy back then. It was an ordinary market town, on the cusp of changing into something else. Next door to the shop where Ioan had bought the dictionary, there was an old-fashioned ironmongers, its goods overflowing onto the pavement. Anna remembered buying a scrubbing brush there. Why a scrubbing brush? Why could she remember the brush and its pale wood? The strangest urge came over her to return to Hay to buy a wooden scrubbing brush, and get rid of the blue plastic one she kept under the sink. Would there be such an ordinary and cheap wooden brush for sale there today? But it would be lovely to go there and look for one, and maybe go for a spin down the road to Capel-y-ffin.

The brush and the dictionary had been bought before the days of the famous festival. The first time, the only time, Anna had been to the festival was in 2005. Some English second-homer who came to stay in his cottage in her valley had taken a shine to her, and had suggested the two of them spend a couple of days at Hay Festival. The visit hadn't been a success.

'We need to hurry, Anna. I don't want to miss this talk.'

And she'd acquiesced to his plummy command, drawing away from the shop before she'd had a chance to pick up a scrubbing brush. That night, in a hotel in Hay, was the last time Anna had shared a bed with a man.

The next time the second-homer came to his cottage he had a slim woman by the name of Jessica in tow. The couple came over to Nant yr Aur for coffee, and their Barbour boots left unfamiliar patterns on the slate floor of the kitchen. That was the only time they crossed her threshold, despite coming to stay in the holiday home several times over the years.

That man had also offered to buy Nant yr Aur, the day he and Jessica came over. Strange – Anna could remember her name, a woman she'd only met the once, but couldn't remember his. She stared out of the window, trying to distract herself so the name would surface. Martin! Yes, it was Martin, of course. And Martin had wanted to buy Nant yr Aur, and had elaborated on all the wonderful things he'd do to the house, and how he and Jessica would become part of the local community. Really, they'd be an asset to the place, broadening people's horizons.

'I've no wish to sell.'

And him still banging on trying to persuade her. Anna sitting quietly, and eventually Jessica interrupting him and quietly pointing out that Anna had already given him an answer and perhaps he should learn to listen more. That was probably why Anna remembered her name, because of that.

She was thankful Siôn had accepted that she had no wish to sell, and had not harped on about it. It would have been difficult to enjoy his company for a whole afternoon, had he insisted on turning the conversation to the subject of selling Nant yr Aur at every opportunity. If he had, she certainly wouldn't have asked him to call again. Nor suggested that next time he should come for supper. So that's why I waxed the best table, she thought.

9

ANNA ADDED ONE MORE THING TO THE SHOPPING LIST BEFORE giving it to Emyr. She watched him read through it, and saw him smile as he suppressed the urge to ask. She put him out of his misery.

'I've invited someone to supper.'

He nodded. 'Limes are those green lemons, eh? If there aren't any, do you want me to fetch a lemon?'

'Yes. Use your common sense. So long as there's meat and bread and wine. Thanks, Emyr. I won't be in this plaster for much longer.'

Emyr pushed the list and the money into his pocket and made to go. With his hand on the latch he turned back to her and asked, 'Anyone I know?'

'No, I don't think so. I've only just met him myself.'

They looked at each other for a moment.

'And before you start spreading gossip, I'm old enough to be his mother.'

'I wasn't ... See you this afternoon.'

It was no surprise that Emyr was keen to know more.

Anna couldn't remember the last time she'd officially invited someone to supper at Nant yr Aur. Offering a bite to eat to someone who was there anyway was what she usually did. But the sort of question she'd asked Siôn – 'Would you like to come for supper on Wednesday night?' – hadn't crossed her lips in years. And so she'd have to do other unfamiliar things, including deciding what to cook. She realised she should have asked Siôn if he ate meat. She had no phone number to ring and ask him. She'd decided that he looked like a meat-eater. And young lads like puddings, she'd thought, so she'd have to make pudding. That was when she'd added 'dark chocolate and a tin of crème de marrons' to the list for Emyr. Before he'd arrived she'd scribbled 'try Linor's shop'.

The pudding recipe came from Ioan. She could remember every detail of the first time she'd eaten it – the plates, the jug for the cream, and the chocolate kisses that turned into riotously silly lovemaking before coming back to the table to finish pudding. And Ioan refusing to tell her the recipe for ages, inventing some ancient aunt in Vienna who had disclosed the recipe to him on her deathbed, making him swear to keep the secret forever. She eventually discovered that it was essentially no more than chocolate and a tin of puréed chestnuts, but to them it became Tante Adèle's Pudding from then on.

Anna wondered for the first time if perhaps there was anyone else in the world who knew of Tante Adèle's Pudding. She imagined writing a letter and addressing it to Tante Adèle, Vienna, and explaining that she, Anna, knew about her famous pudding and that she was about to make it for a young man that she'd met only once and who, on some strange whim, she'd invited to supper. She thought of the letter lying, undeliverable, in some post office in Austria before a postman – who wasn't too worried about the rules – opening it one boring afternoon as he waited for his shift to finish. And he would – because she'd have written out the recipe in the letter to check she'd been faithful to it – then go home and make the pudding for his girlfriend. And then two more people would know about Tante Adèle's Pudding. And after a while they'd have little blond children who would know, and someday their children would too, maybe ...

She snatched a sharp knife out of the drawer and started peeling the potatoes. For the pleasure of feeling the knife cutting through their hardness, she peeled far more than were needed. She'd never enjoyed using a proper potato peeler that only peeled off a thin layer of skin. She dropped the peelings into the compost bucket, which was quickly filling up, and let the potatoes stand in cold water in the pan. There was nothing more to do until Emyr returned with her shopping. She went to sit by the fire to try and distract herself from the awful itching under the plaster. She would have given anything to be able to scratch it, but there was no way of reaching it. She tried to lose herself in a book, but the writing wasn't up to much and every sentence or two the itching resurfaced in her consciousness as the most important thing in the world.

Then she realised that she'd read a whole chapter and the itch had subsided. She couldn't say when it had disappeared, and she could scarcely remember how dreadful it was. She was reluctant to think about it in case it reappeared. She shut her eyes for a minute before starting the next chapter.

'Christ, talk about living the life of Riley!'

She smiled at him. She couldn't remember when Emyr had given up knocking at Nant yr Aur. Maybe he had never knocked.

'Thanks. Stick them on the kitchen table.'

'D'you need anything else?'

'Half an hour back I'd have given the world for someone with hands tiny enough to scratch under this plaster.'

Emyr looked at his own spade-like hands, and shook his head. 'Your fire's going out, madam,' he said.

He loaded the stove with wood and went out to the shed to fetch more. By the time he came back Anna was in the kitchen unpacking the shopping. She smiled as she saw there was a lemon *and* a lime. She wasn't even sure if Siôn drank gin, or if he drank alcohol at all, or if he was someone who worried about drinking and driving. But she'd formed a picture in her head of how such an evening should start, and offering him a gin and tonic was in the script. And the stage directions noted: 'music, not too loud, folk or opera'. But, so far, that was all that was written of the drama.

Emyr's voice came from the living room. 'I'll call by in the morning if I get a chance.'

And before Anna could even shout her thanks, she heard the sound of the door closing.

10

'GIN? OR I HAVE ...'

'Gin would be very nice.'

There was silence as Anna poured the gin, poured the tonic, squeezed the ice cubes from their cells and sliced the lime.

'Iechyd da.'

'Cheers.'

And then more silence, as they both sipped their drinks and the voice of Siân James came from somewhere, singing her hiraeth about Meirionnydd.

Anna had never got on with the word 'hiraeth' and all the romantic nonsense attached to it. It was as if the word had taken on a special meaning to Welsh people, but only because it was untranslatable into English. She remembered her pleasure on learning that there was a Portuguese word, saudade, with a very similar meaning. The feeling of hiraeth was not unique to Welsh and Welsh people; it was English people and their language that were odd, deficient.

She had never expressed hiraeth about Nant yr Aur. Never to herself nor to anybody else. She'd say to Ioan, while watching a film in the flat, that she had to go home for a while, and in the beginning he'd question this and refuse to accept it. But later he accepted without demur. And when she'd stayed in the Ariège sunshine for the whole summer fifteen years ago, she'd told herself she had to come back or the garden would be beyond redemption. But when she arrived home the garden was neat and tidy, the grass cut, the weeds under control, the last of the beans ready to harvest. In the hedge next to the wigwam of beans was a blue ball, and there were a few unfamiliar things in the kitchen cupboards. She remembered, for some reason, that there were coriander seeds and a few other spices she didn't ordinarily use, and that more books had disappeared from the shelves. That was almost the only sign that someone had been staying in the house while she'd been away. It was impossible to say how long Ioan had been there. She suspected there'd been someone with him, or at least someone had called – perhaps a friend with a child, and for some reason she imagined it was a little girl with red hair, plaited, who had left her ball behind. She didn't ask Emyr. But while collecting the beans she felt a strong longing for Ioan, felt hiraeth for him. And collecting the last of the beans from the wigwam at summer's end, before pulling up the shrivelled stems and putting them on the compost heap, gave her this bittersweet feeling for a second or two every year.

Anna had set the table in the middle of the afternoon, before going up to wash and change.

'Sit down,' she said to Siôn, gesturing to the chair furthest from the kitchen. And then, almost immediately, she changed her mind. 'No, come with me to the kitchen so you can carry things in.'

He placed his glass of gin between the candlestick and the bread on the table, and followed her through to the back.

'Thank you, dear. It will be so good when this plaster's off. I feel like I'm shackled.'

Anna leaned one of the crutches against the wall for a moment and started to dish out the food onto two white plates that were sitting, waiting, next to the cooker. She placed the chicken pieces on the plates first, then the roast potatoes and lastly a stew of beans and onions and tomatoes.

She saw the look on Siôn's face as he smelled the stew. She saw the half-smile on his face.

'Cumin?' he asked, leaning closer to the plate to smell it properly.

'Yes, and the last of the season's beans from the garden. They've been in the freezer for months.'

'When I was a kid we used to have stew like this, with beans and cumin.'

Siôn picked up both plates and carried them to the oak table in the other room. Anna followed him on her crutches. The two of them ate in silence for a while.

'Siôn? Would you do me another favour?'

He smiled.

'There's a bottle of wine in the fridge. Would you fetch it?'

Siôn came back with the bottle and a corkscrew. He opened the bottle, but let Anna pour it into the glasses.

She hesitated before filling his glass.

'Where do you have to drive to?'

Siôn looked awkward for a moment. 'I've been a bit cheeky. I've pitched my tent over there.' He pointed through the window into the darkness. 'The other side of the river.'

Anna filled his glass, and then filled her own. She swallowed a mouthful of the cold liquid before commenting. 'It's Emyr's land. But he won't mind.'

'He's the old boy with the blue Land Rover?'

'Yes,' Anna replied, suddenly realising that Emyr was now exactly that. 'Have you met him?'

Siôn nodded, with his mouth full of chicken and potatoes.

When, she wondered, had Emyr turned into an old man? Had she turned into an old woman? Of course she was, certainly to someone Siôn's age. But she didn't know when it had happened. Five years ago? Ten years ago? Before that? She looked at the young man opposite her, enjoying his food, and for a moment couldn't understand why she'd invited him. But then Siôn smiled at her and started talking about wind turbines, or wind power stations as he called them. And then the conversation turned to Dylan Thomas and then to cats, and by then they'd finished their food and the wine bottle was empty and the walls of Nant yr Aur were warming up and listening.

'Pudding!'

Anna started, with difficulty, to stand up.

'Sit down, you've gone to enough trouble already. I'll be the waiter tonight.'

Anna lowered herself back down onto the chair and let him put logs on the fire, and go to the kitchen to fetch the pudding from the fridge. He placed the brown circle in front of her and she cut two generous portions and put them in the bowls.

Siôn took a spoonful into his mouth and made an appreciative 'Mmm' sound, like a child. Or like a man.

'Thank you for inviting me, Anna. It's been a lovely evening, just like being at home.'

'Where is home, Siôn?'

He took another piece of Tante Adèle's Pudding before answering her.

'There is no home now. There was never one place anyway – we moved around all through my childhood. And now ...'

He paused and took a mouthful of wine. A second bottle had been opened without the need for discussion.

'And now I'm a little orphan child.' And before Anna had a chance to respond he raised his glass to her. 'Iechyd da, and iechyd da to whoever created the recipe for this amazing pudding.'

11

THE NEXT MORNING ANNA STOOD IN THE KITCHEN IN HER dressing gown, trying to decide which would be better: a large greasy breakfast or half a pint of orange juice and two paracetamols. It took her a couple of seconds to realise that the noise she could hear was a knock at the door.

'Young folks don't get hangovers, from what I remember,' she said under her breath, still fumbling in the cupboard for the paracetamol. She'd decided that grease and juice and chemicals would be the best cure for her headache.

'Come in,' she called out, 'it's open.'

'Yoo-hoo! It's only me!'

Anna groaned when she realised it was Dora.

'Some heifers have got onto the road, and Emyr's had to go straight down there. I told him I'd call to make sure you're alright. He said he'd promised to call in.'

Dora placed a Tupperware box on the table. 'Scones. Thought you'd be having trouble baking these days.'

They both knew that Anna seldom made scones. Anna swallowed the tablets.

'Are you in pain? You should ask the doctor for something stronger, you know.'

'Coffee, Dora?'

Anna drank two glasses of water as she waited for the kettle to boil, half-listening to Dora.

'Did you know that someone's camping the other side of the river? I'll send Emyr over just now to see who they are. Don't you try to go over. I'm not going either. You never know ...'

Anna poured boiling water onto the coffee in the red pot, and let the torrent of words spurt unhindered around the room.

'Do you want anything to eat, Dora? I haven't had breakfast yet.'

She put four slices of bacon in the frying pan, knowing that Dora wouldn't refuse the offer.

'It's a strange time of year to be camping. My goodness, I bet it was cold out there last night.'

Anna felt guilty for not having been more insistent that Siôn should sleep in the house. She'd sort-of offered, but Siôn's response had been very definite.

'I've got good equipment, and it's a sheltered little spot, and I've slept in far worse places.'

Anna had looked at him, expecting more details, but he hadn't elaborated.

'Another time.' And then he'd leaned towards her and brushed a light kiss onto her cheek. 'Goodnight.'

Before going to bed, Anna sat for a long time in front of the dying embers in the stove, drinking the remainder of the third bottle of wine. As she put the glass and the empty bottle on the table, she glanced through the window and saw that there was still a faint light inside the tent. She left the curtains open and a small lamp on so there would be a light in the Nant yr Aur window all night.

She usually did that every time she left Nant yr Aur. Ioan learned to accept the waste of money uncomplainingly, although he never understood her rationale. To be fair, she had only offered an explanation a couple of times. 'It's not for me, you know. I don't need the light. But it shows we're coming back, doesn't it?'

The same impetus held her back from washing every dirty dish before closing the heavy oak door, regardless of whether she was leaving for two hours or two months. Something had to be left half-undone, even if only a novel half-read, straddling the arm of the fireside chair. That was the significant difference she noticed on returning from the months in Ariège fifteen years ago. The tidiness let her know that someone who had no intention of returning had been there.

Dora had finished her bacon sandwich and coffee, and obviously felt she should do something to help poor Anna on her crutches, but then again wasn't sure what to do. Anna gave a silent prayer of thanks that Siôn had insisted on washing up last night, and that there weren't two telltale plates and glasses. As her grandmother would say, 'Easier to shut their eyes than shut their mouths.'

Dora lifted the saucepan lid that covered the remains of the bean stew.

'Something spicy, exotic, eh?'

'Cumin is what you can smell. The rest is nothing more than tomatoes, onions and beans,' answered Anna, pouring herself a third mug of black coffee. And only as she said this did she recall that those beans of fifteen years ago had been left unharvested.

'Would you like me to light the fire for you, Anna?'

By now Dora had wandered into the living room.

'Thanks. Erm, I'm sure there's still some life there. Try putting a few dry sticks from that box on it … Maybe it'll rekindle.'

12

ANNA GRABBED HER CRUTCHES TO SEE DORA OUT. ALL SHE wanted was peace and quiet in which to nurse her hangover; it hadn't been much improved by the grease and coffee and paracetamol.

'The camper's gone! He was down there.'

There was nothing to be seen except the usual rushes and a pair of magpies wrangling in the hawthorn that grew beside a bend in the river. Anna felt a kind of odd emptiness, and a strange disappointment in Siôn's having left without saying goodbye to her. She thanked Dora for dropping by, and said that of course she'd be down to see her and Emyr as soon as the plaster was off and she could drive again.

She stood in the doorway watching the pert little woman getting into her little red car. She remained standing there for a long time, staring at the land on the other side of the river where the tent had been and where there was now nothing to say there had been a tent. The two magpies grew weary of their quarrel, rose from the tree and flew towards her, swerving towards the bird table and then, for some reason, reconsidering and flying higher, disappearing from sight. Anna kicked herself for not asking Dora to refill the bird feeders. Two tits were pecking at a handful of peanuts at the bottom of one of them, and it would soon be empty. But refilling them was too much effort for Anna.

She turned, closed the door behind her, and laboriously climbed back to the bedroom. Purposely avoiding the mirror, she slid back between sheets that had long since turned chilly. The secret of living successfully by yourself, someone had once told her, was learning to appreciate cold patches in the bed. She curled up as best she could, and lay like a child in the womb. Before long, the sheets warmed up and she fell asleep.

When Anna woke up she felt a hundred times better. She moved her head with care, but the dreadful pounding had gone. The nausea had subsided too. She turned to look at the small clock on the bedside table. It showed almost three o'clock in the afternoon, although her body was convinced it was now the next morning, and that she should have breakfast again.

She remembered this disjuncture between her body and the clock after Dylan's death. She would wretchedly wander the house at night, and do all sorts of jobs – cleaning, cooking, painting walls. To start with, Ioan would come and find her if he woke up and realised she wasn't on her side of the bed. She recalled the night he came looking for her and found her weeding rows of beetroot, wearing a head torch like a miner. He lost it with her that night. And she raged back to start with, and then gave in, wailing and letting him lead her back to bed.

But that didn't break the pattern. She would be so tired she'd creep back to bed during the day, or doze under a blanket on the sofa. And Ioan's timetable became more disciplined – he relied on his alarm clock to wake him every morning at six, and went to bed every night the second the ten o'clock news was over. Had the stairs not been so narrow, they would literally have passed each other on them.

Anna remembered waking several times as she had done today, in the middle of the afternoon, alone in the bed, looking at the blue sky through the window and feeling the coldness of the bed close in. Then she'd hear Ioan moving about downstairs and the bed would warm up and she'd go back to sleep.

At some point during this period, Dora had turned up at five o'clock in the morning while Anna was making a huge pan of lobscouse, and intending to make plum jam once the big pan was empty.

'You don't mind, do you? I saw you were up. I couldn't sleep either, and I've been for a walk, and saw your light, and I thought ...'

'Will you have a bowl of lobscouse?'

And the two of them sat at the kitchen table, scoffing down the stew as though they hadn't eaten for days, and Dora was able to pour her heart out. All Anna had to do was listen. She had nothing much to contribute in any case – she hadn't the faintest idea if Emyr was having an affair or not. At the time she had thought he didn't have the balls – that he enjoyed flirting and fantasising and thinking what-ifs, and enjoyed mulling over possibilities. Maybe telling Dora little fibs gave him a bit of a kick, even, along with concealing that he'd had a coffee with a certain woman when he'd been to the mart. But had that woman taken him up, he'd have run home pretty smartish. Anna didn't divulge any of this – just listened, and refilled Dora's bowl with lobscouse.

As Dora finished her second bowlful, they heard Ioan's alarm clock go off, and within a couple of minutes he was in the kitchen, offering to make them toast and coffee. Dora excused herself, stood up, and left. Anna forced herself to eat toast and drink coffee with Ioan. Then she hugged him tightly for a long time, without saying a word, and struggled to stay awake all day and keep him company. When she got to bed, a couple of hours ahead of him, she lay there for a few minutes, looking at the long streaks of clouds illuminated on one side by the moon, acknowledging that she still had some things to be grateful for.

Before long her sleep had slipped back into its old pattern of no pattern, but by then Ioan had started to travel for his work again. Anna never found out – from Dora nor from anyone else – whether or not Emyr had had a relationship with the woman at the mart and that day was forgotten, as were so many others.

13

THE PHONE RANG TWICE THE FOLLOWING DAY, BUT IT WASN'T Siôn. Emyr called by as night was falling and replaced a lightbulb in the kitchen where one that had burned out had left her in the dark. Anna managed to ignore the restlessness that was sending her round the house on her crutches to do things and to do nothing. Despite the mental relief she'd felt when she'd started to draw her pension, on days like these she would have loved to have had a job to go to. Not that she'd ever had an important post, nothing worthy of the description 'career' or 'calling': they were all just 'jobs', and she'd moved from one to the next without any sort of plan. But today it would have been nice to know that she had to get to the cafe or the garden centre by nine, and that her day would be filled with dirty crockery, sacks of compost and the needs of demanding customers.

She could write to Siôn, of course, but she couldn't imagine what she'd put in such a letter. She didn't know what she'd ask him nor what she'd say.

'Tell the truth,' said the small part of Ioan that still loitered within the walls of Nant yr Aur. 'It's much easier.'

So she started to write a letter in her head to Siôn.

Dear Siôn,

I had been expecting to see you before you left the other morning. I hope you will return to Nant yr Aur, because ...

She started to chew the end of the imaginary biro before resuming in her head.

... because your presence in Nant yr Aur felt right.

There was no need for further explanation. Ioan had never preached the need for telling the whole truth. The truth and the truth only – that was his creed. And perceiving the whole truth was pretty hard. It meant burrowing into little holes and sucking out everything there, and looking carefully at each and every thing that had been assembled and cataloguing them and naming them.

But she didn't send the letter, didn't even write it. Siôn wrote to her. Before the end of the week a postcard arrived from Vienna – a picture of white Spanish Riding School stallions – on the reverse, in stylish handwriting, the message: Tante Adèle sends her regards. S x.

Anna laughed – now, at last, there was someone else who knew about Tante Adèle. Although she didn't remember telling him the story. Too much wine, Anna dear, she said. She gazed at the picture of the white stallions and thought about how lovely it would be to go and see them dance.

'And what's stopping you, Anna Morris?' she said aloud, looking accusingly around the room. She saw her Karrimor rucksack lying dirty and full of holes beside the stove. She'd have to buy another, but that was a small matter.

After the plaster comes off, and I've got my strength back, when the weather's better, and when there's enough money, then I'll go to Vienna or somewhere. Dublin, maybe; no need for a passport to go to Dublin, is there? She wasn't even certain she had a valid passport. She should look; renewing it was bound to take time. She knew her passport, valid or not, was stored safely with the deeds to Nant yr Aur. 'I'll look for it tomorrow,' she said to herself.

There had been some discussion about adding Dylan to her passport, and he had been taken to be photographed. Ioan was keen that they should spend a term with him while he was at the university at Rennes. But they'd had to rethink. Ioan had had to break his contract halfway through the term. Did he ever go back? Was he ever invited back as visiting lecturer for a term? She imagined a female member of some committee in some department suggesting, 'How about we ask that man, the one who had to go home because his son died, what was his name ... Ioan Gwilym?' And someone else enquiring where he was by now, and did anyone happen to know how to get hold of him. And somebody was bound to know where he was.

For a while, Anna forwarded letters on to the flat, but then the postman brought two back, marked with a stranger's handwriting: not known at this address. If she had anything of the detective about her, she could certainly have followed his trail. As she understood it, if she were any good with computers it would be a fairly straightforward matter to track him down. Maybe she'd buy a computer. Not to look for Ioan, but for ... To be honest, she wasn't sure what for. Any more than she was sure if she needed a new passport, even if the old one had expired. Such thoughts were nothing more than an indication of the irritability and restlessness that had been eating away at her for days.

She was putting a drawing pin through the picture of the white stallions, to pin it to the shelf above the sink, when there was a knock, the sound of the door opening and a 'Yoo-hoo!' Anna looked at Emyr and Dora standing side by side in her living room.

'Is something the matter?' she asked.

'No, of course not. We were setting off to buy tiles, and I said to Emyr, "You know what'd be a good idea? That we fetch Anna – I'm sure the poor thing must be suffering from cabin fever by now, and a little outing and lunch in a cafe would do her the world of good" and ...'

Anna caught Emyr's eye for half a second before answering his wife. 'D'you know what, Dora, you're right. Cabin fever is exactly what it is.'

Dora turned triumphantly to her husband. 'I told you so, didn't I. You would have just ...'

But by then Anna had her coat on and Emyr had gone outside to open the Land Rover door. He took her crutches from her and placed them in the back, and then half-lifted her in.

'What on earth do you eat, woman?'

Anna just smiled at him. 'Careful you don't drop me.'

'I wouldn't, you know.'

'I know you wouldn't.'

While the other two were discussing tiles, Anna propelled herself slowly round the superstore on her crutches. With the help of one of the lads who worked there, she bought two tins of yellow paint. She'd decided it wouldn't be a bad idea to cheer up the bathroom. It was high time Nant yr Aur was spruced up – she'd been rather neglectful of the place of late.

14

ANNA HAD NEVER BEEN ABLE TO LEAVE A NEW TIN OF PAINT unopened for long. She shoved a small chisel under the lip of the lid in two places, then carefully lifted it. 'Sweet Sunshine' was the colour. There was bound to be someone somewhere, maybe an entire team of workers, who did nothing but invent names for different colours of paint. Maybe it was a bit chicken-and-egg? Did the creator of the paint, of the colour, present a new colour to the naming panel and await its baptism, so that it would no longer be known as 'Yellow 266'? Or maybe it was the creatives who decided the public would buy something named 'Sweet Sunshine', and it was they who went to the laboratory and said, 'Please let us have a new yellow, not too dark and not too bright.' The world was full of things she knew nothing about, things she would never know anything about.

Leaning on one crutch, she lifted the tin of paint off the floor and placed it on the edge of the bath. She dipped her brush in the paint and spread a little onto the bathroom wall. She considered it for a minute and then did the same thing on another part of the wall, beside the window. She contemplated. Yes, it pleased her, and was an improvement on the blue which had looked like the sea on a summer's day when selected, but which now gave the place a cold feel, like the watery eyes of an old man. She fetched old newspapers from the kitchen, carrying them tucked under her arm to the bathroom, and spread them across the floor. Then she fetched the little radio. She smiled. A month ago, it would have been totally impossible for her to do something like this. Making a cup of tea had been a challenge then. Now she could put a little weight on the leg. Things were improving. She carefully painted her way round the room, moving clockwise. As she reached any impediment – curtains, a shampoo bottle, socks drying on the radiator – she threw them higgledy-piggledy into the bath. She knew that most people – Dora, Ioan, her father – clear everything out of a room before they start painting. And then they wash the walls with sugar soap, fill the holes with Polyfilla, and rub down the walls and woodwork with sandpaper. But Anna was painting like her mother ...

Two hours later she'd been round the whole room, and was delighted with the change. She rested on the edge of the bath. That she'd succeeded was a miracle, but she wasn't stupid enough to consider standing on a chair. This meant there was no way for her to reach the highest foot or so of wall. She had known from the outset that this would be a problem, but she had faith there would be some way round it. Maybe someone would call round, or maybe she'd just have to leave a strip of sea beyond the yellow beach for a fortnight, until the plaster was off.

She looked again at the blue border. If the handle of her brush was a touch longer ... 'Clever girl!' she said aloud to herself. She gripped her crutches and went to fetch the broom and look for string. She was in the process of tying the paint brush to the broom handle – and spattering her jeans still further with the Sweet Sunshine – when there was a knock at the door.

'It's open!'

She heard the door open and whoever was there hesitate.

'I'm up here!'

She held firm to the string lashed round the two brush handles, and looked towards the door. There stood Siôn, half-smiling as he studied the incomplete paint job. He dropped his bag to the floor.

'Can you manage making a cup of tea?'

'Yes, of course.'

'May I use this chair?'

He took the paint brush from her, letting the string unwind.

'I'll have finished this by the time the kettle boils.'

Anna left him to it without further discussion; she went down to the kitchen and filled the kettle. She smiled as she heard a tenor voice penetrating through the walls from the bathroom.

'You are my sunshine, my only sunshine ...'

And to her surprise, after finishing the chorus he started on the first verse:

'The other night dear, as I lay sleeping, I dreamt I held you ...' and on through the whole song.

Anna was sitting in the kitchen, starting to drink her tea, before Siôn came down. She looked at him washing the paintbrush and then washing his hands. A hint of late afternoon sun came in through the circle of stained glass that hung in the window and created a pattern on his shoulder.

'I'm never sure,' said Anna, 'whether that's a happy song or a sad one.'

'Sad,' said Siôn, pouring tea from the blue teapot. Anna nodded, and nudged a packet of chocolate biscuits closer to him. She pointed at the picture of the white stallions above the sink.

'Right, I want to hear all about Vienna ...'

Anna realised – after Siôn had vacated his chair, thanked her for the tea, promised to come round again the day after tomorrow, and left – that she'd had the whole story of the trip to Vienna. Every detail, from the smell of the stallions' stables to the colour of the cakes in the shops; from a long, entertaining story about two children misbehaving in a shoe shop to the colour of the curtains in the hotel. Every detail – except why he'd gone, and whether he'd had company or not.

***

Siôn kept his word and came back late in the afternoon two days later. Late enough for Anna to have decided that he wasn't coming, and to start thinking she'd imagined he'd said it. Then, when he turned up soaking wet, feeling guilty that she'd doubted him and guilty that keeping his word had been important enough to him to merit walking there in the rain.

'You're soaked through. Go and have a shower. There's plenty of hot water, and towels. Maybe there's clothes that'll fit you too.'

Anna liked the way Siôn took up her offer without any fuss, setting his bag down carefully beside the table. She went to burrow into the airing cupboard to retrieve a pair of jeans that had been there for decades, and lingered to listen to the singing coming from the bathroom. She left the jeans and one of her largest T-shirts on the floor outside the door and went downstairs, where she could no longer hear the lyrics of 'Rescue Me', only some shiver through the stones of the house that told her he was still singing and that the song had changed. Was Fontella Bass still alive? She had no idea. One more thing she didn't know.

Anna turned her head suddenly and looked up at the landing. Siôn was standing there looking at her, and she had the feeling he'd been standing there a while. She almost felt he'd willed her to turn round. Siôn pulled on the T-shirt and grabbed the towel, rubbing his hair dry as he walked downstairs towards her.

15

SIÔN WALKED BAREFOOT ACROSS THE KITCHEN FLOOR, AND Anna found herself staring at his feet and smiling.

'Here you go – a jumper as well.'

Siôn draped the wet towel on the back of a chair and put on the jumper. He pulled a laptop from his bag.

'I've come to show you the pictures.'

He put the laptop on the pine table and opened it. Without discussion, Anna opened a bottle of red wine and placed it, along with two glasses, on the table. She sat down beside him and looked at photo after photo of his trip to Vienna.

There was a young woman in several of the pictures.

'Your girlfriend?' asked Anna eventually, when Siôn offered no explanation.

'No, my sister. Mali.'

'I didn't know you had a sister. She's pretty.'

'Half-sister,' answered Siôn, as if that explained something. But Anna couldn't tell whether it explained the fact that he hadn't mentioned her until now, or explained the fact that she was pretty.

In the next photo, Mali was seated at a table in a cafe chatting with a smartly dressed middle-aged woman. The shoes, bag and beret of the woman all matched, and a small white dog lay at her feet.

'Tante Adèle,' said Siôn and laughed. 'We didn't find out her real name, but Mali and I were convinced she was Tante Adèle. Or, rather, Tante Adèle's daughter: the old woman is no longer with us, of course.'

'But Tante Adèle didn't have a daughter. That's why she passed the recipe on to Ioan,' answered Anna, playing along with the conceit.

'She was in Australia when her mother died. That was why she was chatting with us. She wanted to relearn the family recipe.'

'And did you remember it?'

'Of course. But we refused to tell her.' Siôn clicked the mouse to move on to the next shot – a back view of the woman in her black coat and her red bag and beret and shoes, walking down a narrow street with the little white dog at her heels. Siôn chuckled. 'Look, she's walking off in a huff.'

Anna poured more wine, slopping some as she laughed.

'Will you stay for a bite to eat?' It wasn't really a question. 'I've put clean sheets on the bed in Dylan's bedroom ...' The words felt awkward in her mouth.

And that was when she explained about Dylan. It was late by the time they ate, and later still when Siôn went to bed, leaving Anna sitting alone in front of the fire. She sat there, totally still and quiet in the chair, listening to the sound of someone moving about in another part of the house, and trying to remember the last time that had happened. For a moment, the urge came over her to run upstairs and ask him to sleep in her bedroom, and she would sleep in the single bed; or, better still, leave the little bed empty and she'd sleep on the sofa. She reached for the bottle of whisky and the urge disappeared, replaced by a kind of warm feeling.

She didn't think anyone had slept in Dylan's room since he'd died. That fact came as a shock to her. She was certain it wasn't a deliberate decision on her part. One or two friends had been to stay in the early years, and they had sensitively chosen to sleep on the sofa rather than in a bedroom full of toys. But then the toys had been disposed of, white paint now covered the blue and the curtains had been replaced years ago. But by that time no one came to stay overnight. And Anna hadn't had to consider how she felt about having another person sleep in Dylan's room. Until tonight.

If I had moved house, she thought, none of this would be relevant. She remembered the day – a few years after she'd learned that she was Nant yr Aur's sole owner – when she had gone down into town, and walked past the windows of three estate agents, trying to decide between them. She went back to the first one, because that one's door was painted a cheerful red and had a shiny brass door knob. She walked in and smiled hesitantly at the young girl behind the desk.

'I'd like to sell my house.'

The girl smiled at her and invited her to sit down opposite. They made all the arrangements, and a date was agreed upon for 'Steve – he's the one who visits all the properties' to come over. The girl explained that Steve would have to measure the rooms, take photographs and create an attractive description of the property.

'We tend to avoid the word "remote" these days. "Secluded" sounds so much better, doesn't it?'

They smiled at each other again.

Then Anna went home and sat on the doorstep without opening the door. Although she'd given up smoking the moment she'd realised she was pregnant, an overwhelming urge for one of her teenage cigarettes overcame her. She was conscious of the perfect arch of stone above her head, those stones slotted edgewise, looking as if they could slip free so easily, yet not one of which could move out of place. She stood up, put her hand on the latch – and felt a wave of relief as it moved easily and the door swung open. She went straight to the phone and explained that there would be no need for Steve to come, that she'd changed her mind. Anna assured the girl with the smile – she could even see the smile over the phone – that she would be sure to get in touch with them if the situation changed. Then she went to bed, even though it was only five in the afternoon.

Yes, she had considered selling since then – when money was tight; when the winters were long and wet; when she looked at the skin of her hands and realised that she was getting old and hadn't been anywhere or done anything; and twice in the past when she'd been offered good money for it. But all she'd had to do was to remember that day, sitting on the doorstep, the fear that the door of Nant yr Aur would, once again, be closed to her for years, as it had been before she'd met Ioan, and she would run her hand down the nearest wall and forget the idea.

She corrected herself – she'd had three offers for Nant yr Aur, of course. It was odd that Siôn's offer had slipped her mind. It was as if the gentleman who'd written the letter to her weeks ago wasn't the same person as the young man who was now sleeping upstairs. Neither of them had said a word about the letter. For a moment, Anna felt as if she were about to be sick. Eating late, mixing the grape and the grain, she said to herself. But she knew that wasn't it.

She walked upstairs slowly and paused beside Dylan's bedroom door. There wasn't a sound. The stupid thought came into her head that Siôn was an apparition. But she knew he would be there in the morning, and she decided she'd break with him then. He was nothing to her, and if he was living in hope of her changing her mind, he was wasting his time. She gave in to temptation, opening the door slowly and softly. She gazed at his curly hair on the pillow, and stood there for a while, listening to the sound of someone else's breathing.

16

ANNA GOT UP BEFORE SIÔN. SHE COULD HEAR HIM SNORING lightly as she passed the bedroom door, and let him sleep. She was still too sleepy to try and make sense of the strange mixture of drunken thoughts that had swamped her brain the previous night, and having a solitary cup of tea would be nice. She'd only just put the kettle on when Emyr walked in.

'You okay?'

'Yeah. Why? And good morning to you too.'

'Saw the light on in the other bedroom late last night.'

'Cup of tea, Emyr?' she said, turning away from him. Then she took pity on him. 'There was someone staying here.'

Before she could explain further, Siôn walked into the room. Anna placed the teapot carefully in the centre of the table.

'Siôn, Emyr. Emyr, Siôn.'

It was only after saying this she remembered Siôn had told her that he'd met Emyr. She looked at their faces, both smiling in a friendly but slightly formal fashion at each other. Maybe he hadn't said he'd already met Emyr. She occasionally doubted her own memory these days, unsure if something had happened or not. As a child, she'd often had strong feelings of déjà vu. This was almost the opposite. She would think something, or even say something, and then be almost immediately convinced she'd imagined it.

She cut two more slices of bread to make toast, and looked again at the two of them sitting at the table. No, there was nothing to suggest they knew each other.

'You're responsible for Siôn being here, you know, Emyr. D'you remember posting a letter for me a while back? Siôn had made an offer to buy the place.'

'Refused my offer, she did!' said Siôn with a smile, reaching for a slice of toast and spreading it thickly with butter and marmalade.

Emyr stirred sugar into his tea thoughtfully. 'What would a young lad like you want with a remote place like this?'

Anna continued pottering about with her back to them, listening. Emyr's voice was totally devoid of emotion. There was no judgement or ridicule in the question, merely a genuine enquiry. Siôn chewed his toast for a moment before answering.

'Sometimes someone takes to a place for reasons that aren't necessarily practical ones. And I've just come into some money ...'

Anna dried a cup agonisingly slowly. She longed for Emyr to question Siôn further. She must have wanted him to ask or she wouldn't have referred to the letter. No, she didn't want him to enquire further. If she'd wanted to know more about Siôn's motives she would have asked him herself, wouldn't she?

'Fair enough,' said Emyr ruminatively. 'I should think it's like with women – you find yourself drawn to one in particular for the oddest reasons. And then ...'

He paused. Anna decided that she didn't want all this philosophising in her kitchen first thing in the morning.

'Can I ask you two to do me a favour, as you're here together? Could you move the bench that's at the bottom of the garden and put it in the shed? I'll give it a coat of paint once it's properly dry. But it's heavy, and it needs two to carry it.'

It was an old bench, with a cast iron frame in the form of ferns at either end and wooden slats connecting them. Ioan had happened to be in some seaside town or other when the council's recreation department were modernising everything; there were dozens of the old benches on the prom, waiting for the scrap man. He had given the workmen a couple of quid and brought the bench home – or at least the cast iron parts – in the back of the car. The slats were replaced and the whole thing painted dark green.

It needed repainting every three years or so, and it had been a tradition from day one that it should be painted a different colour each time. There was no significance to the colour chosen. It had been black for a while, a few years back, because Emyr had been painting the railings of the chapel and there was some paint left over. Anna remembered how grateful she'd been for that black paint. Although she'd been working at the garden centre at the time, money had been tight. She couldn't have explained why the blue paint peeling off the bench, and she with no money to repaint it, had pained her so much – but it had. After the paint dried, she and Emyr sat in the sun on the smart black bench with a glass of elderflower wine each.

'To Our Redeemer, and his black railings!'

'Our Redeemer!'

The glasses were clinked, and the two of them sat in silence for a while, sipping the wine.

'You should come to chapel, Anna.'

'Should I? Why?'

'Because ...'

'You go out of habit. You go to keep Dora company. And Dora goes because she likes singing.'

'Maybe you're right.'

And that was where the conversation was left. Anna wasn't sure if Emyr still went to chapel. She didn't know if Siôn went to chapel or church. She turned, thinking to ask them. But they'd both gone, they had got up quietly and left the table. Anna sat down at the empty table where Siôn had been sitting, poured half a lukewarm cup for herself, and stared at the crumbs in front of her.

17

ANNA RAISED HER HEAD AND LOOKED OUT OF THE WINDOW. She could see the two men carrying the bench up to the shed. They were facing each other – Emyr backing slowly as he knew the lie of the land, and Siôn at the lower end, taking more of the weight. She'd have to get paint, but there was no rush – the bench needed to dry out first. It wasn't the right time to paint it anyway. It should have been done long before she'd had her fall. Or even a year ago.

She decided to leave it to Siôn to decide on the colour this time. Or maybe she'd ask Emyr. Emyr had more of a right. He'd sat on the bench countless times. If the weather was fine, they tended to go and sit on the bench at the bottom of the garden, out of sight, in the days when she was pleased to have company and he was pleased the company was quiet.

Anna realised that hadn't happened for years – every relationship changes, she thought, or maybe it was just that drinking their tea in the kitchen appealed more to two people who were growing older.

The two men came back into the kitchen with satisfied looks on their faces.

'Another cuppa?' asked Anna, moving to refill the kettle.

'No, I'm going to make a move, thanks, Anna.'

Siôn lifted his bag from the floor, and before she could say more than, 'Cheerio, then,' to him he was gone. Emyr stood in the middle of the kitchen as if he couldn't decide what to do next.

'You'll have another cup of tea?'

It was a statement, rather than a question, and Emyr sat down at the table once more, grateful that the decision had been made for him. Anna pushed the sugar bowl closer to him and poured herself another cup.

'Well?' said Emyr after a minute or two.

'Well, what?'

Anna could see Emyr hesitate, searching for the right words.

'You've taken a shine to that young man?'

'Yes. He's a good lad.'

Then Anna looked across the table and gazed at the thick fingers playing with the spoon in the sugar bowl – mounding the grains up and then spreading them out, before re-mounding and re-spreading. The fuzz of hair on his arm, between shirt and wrist, was turning white. Here sat Emyr. And there'd never, ever been a secret between them.

She started trying to explain the muddle of wild thoughts that had run through her head the previous night. She realised this wouldn't make sense to Emyr without the bare facts of what had occurred first – Siôn's letter, the day he'd first called on her, the fact that neither of them had said a word after that day about his offer to buy Nant yr Aur. Her tea grew cold as she talked. Emyr rose to make a fresh pot. Once he'd sat back down and put sugar in his tea, Anna moved the sugar bowl out of his reach.

'Give over, will you.'

'Do you want to sell?'

'No. You know full well that this is where I'll end my days.'

'But?'

'But what?'

Emyr reached for the sugar and put a tiny, tiny extra amount in his tea to justify starting to play with it once more. He looked carefully at Anna's face.

'There is a *but*, though, isn't there?'

'I enjoy his company, I like having him here. If I wasn't here, I'd like to think ...'

She didn't go any further. She wasn't going to say the thing that she hadn't even thought of until a moment ago.

'Yes, well, just be careful, Anna.'

'Careful?'

'I don't want you to get hurt. That's all.'

Emyr ran the spoon over the surface of the sugar until it was completely level.

'I'd better get going. I'll come by tomorrow.'

Anna didn't reply. Only smiled and let the words 'I'll come by tomorrow' linger in her head. How many times had Emyr said those words in this kitchen? He had never said them without keeping his word.

It had been a daily 'I'll come by tomorrow' at one time. Not straight after Dylan's death, but a few years later when Ioan was around less and less often, and everyone else thought the worst grief was over. But Emyr would think of some flimsy excuse to call at some point every day, and Anna would be shamed out of her bed at the sound of the approaching Land Rover. He never said a word about the dirty pots in the sink or that she would be wearing the same clothes as the previous day, and the day before or that it was obvious that the cat hadn't been fed. But Anna knew he noticed. Twmffat was the cat's name, a big tabby tomcat whose role was supposed to be that of mouser. But as the mice didn't present themselves to him, and didn't lie docilely in his bowl, they were perfectly safe.

She wondered if Emyr decided on whether he intended to come over the next day or not before speaking, and would then tell her. Or did he let the words come out of his mouth almost by accident – I'll be over tomorrow, I'll see you soon, I'll be sure to pop by before the end of the week – and then keep his word? There was an important difference between the two things, Anna was sure of that, yet she couldn't put her finger on exactly what the difference was or why it was important. All she knew was that she could rely on Emyr.

18

THE LIST OF THINGS ANNA INTENDED TO DO, ONCE THE plaster was off and the crutches dispensed with, was growing longer by the day. Nothing big or dramatic, but the everyday things she liked doing but which were beyond her. The two crutches that accompanied her everywhere had developed their own character, shifting from being a supporting partnership in the beginning to being two old bitches mocking her.

She remembered once going to Holywell with Ioan, and seeing all the crutches left beside Saint Winifred's Well by the lame who had been cured over the years. There were dozens and dozens of wooden crutches, and one pair of modern metal ones in their midst. Although probably more uncomfortable than the ones she had, having wooden crutches would have been fun. At least they could have ended their days burned on the fire. They could be sawn into handy lengths and tossed into the middle of the flames and be watched turning to ash.

Dylan was a very small baby the day they went to Holywell, a little baby in perfect health, being carried on her breast in a bright orange sling. When Anna bent over to put her fingers in the healing waters of the well, she deliberately sprinkled him with a few drops. She recalled how the water's chill had made him open his eyes for a second before going straight back to sleep. She was aware of Ioan watching her, itching to utter the word 'superstition'. Maybe he had been right, or maybe it had been that poor Winifred had given the little one health for a year or two.

Number goodness-knows-what on the list – go on an outing to Holywell. The next item on the list, definitely, was to get her hair cut. It needed cutting, but she'd designated this as not important enough to ask Emyr or Dora for a lift to the salon she'd been using for a decade or more; ignoring the need had, of course, made it loom even larger in her mind. Maybe there would be a salon in Holywell. She imagined herself striding along the pavement towards a salon where no one knew her, and the staff there doing something different with her hair. Even dyeing it.

She put the kettle on to boil, although she didn't really want any tea. Sometimes boiling the kettle attracted people, and today was one of those rare days when Anna longed for some company. But no one came – no blue Land Rover, no walker in a red coat. She went to the doorway, but there wasn't even one of the Ty'n Giât lads out in the fields for her to wave to.

'Bad sign, Anna Morris,' she said to herself. 'It's a sign of old age when you call men who are nudging thirty "lads".'

She went back to the kitchen table and drank her tea alone, and tried to get into a so-so novel. She felt cross with the author for packing it with stereotypes. It was patently obvious what was going to happen, and Anna couldn't be bothered to carry on reading. She gave thanks that she had very few days like this. And gave thanks that she was capable of seeing that this day was an exception.

A vague memory of childhood came to her. She could hear a friend of her mother's saying that tomorrow they'd have a place in the sun, and then the pair of them laughing when Anna interrupted to say the man on the radio had promised rain.

Anna closed the novel without bothering to mark her place, and switched on the radio. She drifted into the esoteric lull of the Shipping Forecast. '... Lundy, Fastnet, Irish Sea. Mainly east or northeast 4 or 5, occasionally 6. Slight or moderate, occasionally rough ... rain later ...' That came to an end and was followed by a play that succeeded in drawing Anna into an imaginary world. By the time she was released back into reality, she could see that the crutches were nothing but bits of aluminium and plastic.

19

SIÔN ARRIVED A WEEK LATER, HIS BAG ON HIS BACK AS USUAL. For a moment Anna was surprised there was now an 'as usual' but she let the surprise dissipate. In his arms Siôn carried a cat carrier made of pink plastic, and the most unearthly sound was coming from it. He put the carrier down on the floor, ignoring the protests of its displeased tenant.

'Someone I know is looking for a home for her; he's got too many cats as it is. It's difficult for me to look after a cat this year, but I was thinking ...'

'Thinking what?' said Anna, bending down as best she could to look through the pink bars of the carrier's door. Siôn didn't reply.

'Quite young, is she?'

Siôn replied this time. 'Six months. But she's house trained.'

There was silence between them for a while, and the cat had settled into making no more than strangled grumbles under its breath.

'She's half-Burmese,' explained Siôn. 'That's why she's making such a din.'

As Anna straightened up she heard both her knees click. She filled the kettle and set it to boil.

'Does she have a name?'

'Maria,' answered Siôn, relaxing slightly.

Anna closed the kitchen door and the little window above the sink, knocking the circle of stained glass and making it dance gently.

'You'd better let her out, hadn't you?'

The door of the carrier was opened and the cat fell quiet. But she didn't move a muscle, just sat there quietly. Siôn bent over, ready to pull her out.

'Leave her be, Siôn. It's better if she comes out in her own time. Ignore her.'

***

They sat for half an hour before the cat ventured out of the carrier. And then, as she was stepping very slowly and cautiously, feeling every slate slab of the kitchen floor with her paws, Siôn's phone rang in his bag. He dived for it, and in so doing startled the cat. Her explorations had taken her too far from the carrier to jump back into it, and she took one big leap, landing on top of the cupboard beside the cooker. She sat there with her eyes blazing.

'Hello. How are you?'

Anna rarely listened to Siôn's phone conversations.

'Well, Maria darling. D'you think you'll be happy here? It's not bad, you know. But I'll never know how he knew. He's read my mind.'

Anna continued to talk quiet nonsense to the cat, watching her gradually relax. She heard Siôn reassuring whoever was on the other end of the phone that he thought everything would be all right and that he would phone that evening. Then Siôn put the phone back in his bag and turned to face Anna and the cat.

'If you like, I can offer her a home in maybe a year, but I was hoping she could stay here for a while.'

'We'll see, shall we? She'll be okay here. And maybe you'll decide to stay, eh, Maria, my darling?'

The cat folded her paws decorously under herself and stayed on top of the cupboard, watching the strange people below her talking.

Anna could remember Dylan separating himself off like this, going to sit at the other end of the room when the adults were talking round the table. The image Anna had in her head was some occasion when Emyr and Dora had come for supper. This period didn't last long, even though they ate in the kitchen, not at the oak table. Dylan liked eating in company but at the end of the meal the adult conversation was beyond him, no one was taking much notice of him, but on the other hand he wouldn't go into the next room and play with his toys. He would squat down with his back against the wall and watch them, listening without understanding. Emyr would notice him first and would offer to play cars with him or read him a story. But maybe it was Emyr who tired of the adult conversation first. He would leave the table and go to the child on the floor, but despite appearing to be wholly absorbed in the task of lining up all Dylan's toy cars in neat rows, Anna knew that Emyr, like Maria on top of the cupboard, was watching and listening.

The cat took a long time deciding what to do. It was only after Siôn had left and Anna had moved into the other room that she ventured down from the cupboard. But once she was down, she walked with total confidence out of the kitchen in search of Anna. Anna was raking the ashes out from under the grate into a shallow plastic box, but the unfamiliar mewing distracted her.

'D'you think you'll be happy in Nant yr Aur, Maria? It's a good place, y'know.'

The cat looked at her sceptically.

'Yes, food. He didn't think of that, did he? Men! Nor that I'll have to keep you in for a week. But we'll manage.'

Anna looked at the box full of ashes.

'I hope you'll make sense of what this ash is for. And I hope you're ready to eat tuna for a couple of days.'

With the tip of her crutch she shoved the box into a corner of the room. She went back to the kitchen, opened a tin of tuna and tipped it into a saucer. Maria walked up to it, sniffed, and turned and walked away before leaping back on top of her cupboard and looking accusingly at Anna.

'Tuna or mouse or starve, mate.'

But the cat had closed her eyes and had stopped listening to Anna. Ioan could do that. When he did really listen, there was no better listener in the world. He would focus his attention on Anna, asking a question every so often, a question that showed he had been listening attentively. He rarely offered an opinion, unless the subject of the conversation had something directly to do with him. Answering his brief questions would enable Anna to see the inconsistency or unjustness of a position, or any unforeseen snags.

But if she were to discuss something Ioan was not inclined to discuss, or if someone else was discussing something which bored him, he would close his eyes, often literally. He wouldn't get up and move away. He didn't need to – he could absent himself mentally to a place where no one could touch him.

This aspect of Ioan's character never bothered Anna. In common with everyone who has had an unhappy childhood, she had long mastered this skill herself. And for this reason, it was no threat to her to see Ioan occasionally choosing, successfully, not to listen. In any case it didn't happen often, at least not in the early years.

20

DORA PHONED EARLY THE NEXT MORNING. SHE WAS GOING shopping. Did Anna want anything? It was no trouble at all but, sorry, she didn't have time to come up to collect Anna and take her with her, and in any case she had promised to call in on ...

Anna listened or, rather, didn't listen to all the details about what Dora intended to do that morning. When the flow ceased – and she knew that had happened when Dora repeated the original question – Anna asked her if she'd mind fetching a few tins of cat food.

'But you haven't got a cat, Anna. Why d'you want cat food? And what sort?'

'Yes, I have got one. And as far as I know she'll eat any sort of cat food. Thanks very much, Dora.'

Anna replaced the phone in its cradle, whispering 'give me strength' to herself. And then remembered that she now had someone else in the house to talk to. Or at least someone to listen to her. The yellow eyes stared from the top of the cupboard without showing any emotion as Anna expressed her opinion about Dora's form and character.

'Her heart's in the right place, though.'

Anna threw the tuna, which was starting to dry out, into the compost bin.

'And she'll have brought you some cat food by the end of the day. Will you have some milk?'

Dora arrived long before the day's end. Anna was just finishing her lunch. She'd boiled herself an egg, and after eating it had turned the shell upside down in the egg cup so it looked as if it hadn't been touched. She turned the shell back the right way up on hearing Dora yoo-hooing through the door.

'I've brought a couple of tins of cat food, a box of dry food, and a few of those little sachets. You didn't know what she was used to, you said, and cats can be pretty finicky and—'

'Cup of tea, Dora?'

Dora sat down at the table and while the kettle came to the boil Anna tipped some of the cat biscuits into a saucer. It was obvious the sound was familiar to Maria – she jumped down from her cupboard, walked over to her saucer and began to eat greedily. Anna noticed Dora smiling.

'You've obviously made the right choice,' she said to her.

The smile widened.

'I do sometimes.'

For a moment, the voice didn't completely match the smile. Anna got to hear every detail of Dora's trip to town, and a story about two grandsons, and some complication about a jersey she was knitting one of them. But she knew from the outset that there was something else on Dora's mind. She sat patiently and drank too much tea.

'Does Emyr seem himself to you, Anna?'

Anna felt a sort of hard, cold lump somewhere at the bottom of her lungs. The thought that Emyr might be unwell unseated something deep in her core. She remembered him catching flu once, years ago, and remembered him breaking his wrist loading an unruly bullock. But that was all.

'Is he ill?'

'Goodness, no, his body's fine.'

Dora gazed through the window for a minute before continuing.

'But something's bothering him.'

To their surprise, Maria abandoned her saucer and jumped onto Dora's lap.

'You know it's your Auntie Dora who's bought you nice food, don't you. You're lucky, my lady, this one with her crutches can't go anywhere. Has he said anything to you, Anna? I know he sometimes talks to you about things he'd never discuss at home.'

'No,' Anna answered carefully, and realised that she hadn't seen Emyr for a while, not since the day he and Siôn had carried the bench up the garden for her. 'What makes you think something's bothering him?'

'Nothing. Everything.'

Dora stroked the cat until it unsheathed and sheathed its claws into the fabric of her skirt with pleasure.

'I just know,' she added quietly.

Anna promised to let Dora know if Emyr said anything to her. She was amazed at how easy it had always been for her to promise things to Dora without any intention of doing them. But as she watched the little red car with its two green cushions on the parcel shelf drive away, she felt a slight pang of envy about that quiet 'I just know'.

She recognised that there were decades of difference between that and the love and trust there had been between her and Ioan. For an absurd half-second, she felt anger towards a little boy who had died, because he'd killed something else.

She turned back to the cat.

'Maybe she's wrong about Emyr, eh?'

The yellow eyes on top of the cupboard had no opinion on the matter.

'And if there's something worrying him, it's me he'll tell. Sooner or later this is where he'll come to get it off his chest.'

Maria closed her eyes and Anna turned her eggshell upside down once more. She lifted the teaspoon, where a smear of yolk was coagulating, and smashed the empty shell into tiny pieces.

21

IN THE END, ANNA ARRANGED A TAXI AND BERATED HERSELF for pondering so long over what to do. She wasn't going to phone Emyr and Dora. After the conversation she and Dora had had a few days ago, there was a stubborn little germ of suspicion in her head that Emyr was avoiding her. And yet that was silly. She justified her decision not to ask them on the basis that if Emyr couldn't take her, then Dora would offer to, and having Dora fussing and wittering the whole time in the hospital would drive her up the wall. And she wasn't going to ask for an ambulance for all sorts of reasons – far too much drama being the main one. So she phoned and arranged for a taxi to collect her and deliver her to the door of the hospital.

She was there longer than expected. There had to be an X-ray of the leg before the plaster could come off. That's what the young Irishman said – no, she corrected herself, Dr Tóibín was a middle-aged Irishman. Anna looked over his shoulder at the pictures of her own leg. Everything looked grand, he said to her, and the crack in the bone looked fully repaired. Anna was thankful it had been a straightforward break. As he'd searched to locate her X-ray images on his computer screen, she'd caught a glimpse of someone else's X-ray. A leg, and she'd seen that a tiny pin held that person's leg bone together. She was pleased that wasn't her. She looked again at the image of her own bones.

And then a jolly nurse came – this time it was a young man – to remove the plaster and throw it unceremoniously into a rubbish bin, and Anna could see her leg for the first time in weeks. The skin was white and dry.

'That'll be more comfortable for you – but no dancing just yet!' said the nurse mischievously. Anna shoved the sheet of instructions into her pocket.

And that was that. Depending less on the crutches, Anna walked out of the room and down the corridor. Her leg felt strange. She made a phone call to arrange for the taxi to collect her, and went to have a cup of tea in the cafe near the entrance. To celebrate, she asked for a small chocolate cake, and went to sit at a table in the corner with her back to the wall. She longed to be back home. All she wanted to do, before it got dark, was to walk round the house – literally around it. Turn to the right out of the door, and walk clockwise until she was back at the door. It had been impossible to do with the plaster on her leg. Or at least she didn't want to chance it then. There was a place at the back where a rock outcrop and the house met. She remembered explaining, half-seriously, to Ioan.

'That's where the house grew from, you know that, don't you?'

'And when was this?'

'Ages ago, when a good woman needed a home for her family. She sat here, exactly where I am now, and started to describe the house.'

'Helluva shame she forgot to mention a back door.'

'And as she described it, the place grew. And she and her family lived here until ...'

'Until what?'

Ioan was smiling at her, almost laughing. Anna answered him without a trace of a smile on her face.

'I don't know. It must have been something horrendous to make her leave this place – plague and pestilence and betrayal.' Then she relaxed a little. 'Not a word of a lie!'

And tonight, before going to bed, she would walk around Nant yr Aur and sit on the rock that birthed the house in a faraway time, in a period when men didn't deride magic. Having finished her tea, she rose, crumpled the cake wrapper and dropped it into the empty mug, then walked slowly to the main entrance to wait for the taxi.

Although it had been fine when she left Nant yr Aur, by now it was cloudy and the wind was rising. A couple of raindrops struck her cheek as she spotted the red taxi parked neatly opposite the entrance. The driver took her crutches, and she sat in the back of the car, delighting in the warmth, and middle-of-the-road pop music on the radio. She didn't exchange one word with the driver the whole way to Nant yr Aur, and he was startled by the generous tip he received from the silent woman who lived in the middle of nowhere. He thanked her sincerely.

'I'll take the missus out tonight,' he said.

'Yes, do. I hope you have a good night out.'

As she walked to the door she could hear Maria mewing in the house.

'Two minutes, my darling. I've got something I have to do before it gets dark.'

She walked slowly and carefully on her crutches round the house to the back, and lowered herself onto the small rocky outcrop. She sat there with her knees drawn up to her chin, her arms wrapped round her legs. She felt her whole body grow calm. She stared at the house, at the doorless back wall in front of her, and the small window of Dylan's bedroom directly above her, and tried to imagine the spot without the house. She couldn't. It was impossible. In her imagination she pulled the slates off the roof, dismantled every stone of the walls, and pressed them all back into the hillsides from where they'd been quarried. But she stopped almost immediately – the image she'd created in her head made her feel unsettled. And then the rain that had started at the hospital reached Nant yr Aur, and Anna got to her feet. Rather hesitantly she made her way past the rock and continued her circuit of the house until she stood, victorious, at the door.

The door was not locked. She had a key, of course, but she hadn't used it in ages. She opened the door, and closed it quickly behind her before Maria could slip out.

'Maybe tomorrow, darling. You've been inside long enough now, haven't you? And if you decide to go, there's nothing I can do to stop you, is there ...'

She fed the cat and warmed some soup for herself. She was glad she'd been organised enough to make the soup at her own pace the previous day. And, like all soup, it was better reheated. She put a piece of bread and butter in the middle of her bowl to let the butter melt and rise, to appear like eyes on the soup's surface. And then she went to do something else she'd been longing for, but the plaster had prevented – she ran herself a hot bath. She relaxed in the warmth, and derived enormous pleasure from moving her leg and creating little waves. She looked at her toes, at the tap end, and tried to remember a similar image, a picture in which the artist had all sorts of things from her own life floating in the bathwater. Anna had lit candles in the bathroom and had taken a glass of Glenmorangie with her. After finishing that, she went to bed. Maria followed her and curled up on the cold side of the bed.

22

THE NEXT MORNING, ANNA KEPT HER PROMISE AND RELEASED Maria from her house arrest. Not through the door, but through the window above the kitchen sink. It could be left open all the time so the cat could come and go as she pleased. Anna opened the window, then lifted her up and dropped her out through it. Maria landed on the window sill and sat there for a minute, looking through the glass at her prison. Then, before the cat could think of wandering any further, Anna turned away and started to pour cat biscuits into her saucer. Maria had not yet had breakfast. She hesitated for a moment, and then jumped back in through the open window, avoiding the disc of stained glass which was throwing its pattern across everything.

Anna let her eat in peace, and went to sit at the kitchen table with her own breakfast. Through the window she could see one of Emyr's sons moving sheep on the other side of the valley. She looked at the stream of white flowing down the hillside, one sheep breaking free for a moment, and the dogs herding it back to the rest almost without it noticing. Maybe

Emyr had gone over to help with whatever was happening? Perhaps he'd call on his way home from Ty'n Giât.

'We'll make a ginger cake, Maria. What d'you reckon?'

The cat turned to look at her for a second, and Anna knew that if she had shoulders she could shrug, she'd have done so in proper French fashion. The cat left the last biscuit in the saucer, jumped onto the edge of the sink, and from there out through the window.

By the end of the afternoon, Anna had started to worry. There was no sign of Maria nor, for that matter, of Emyr either. It looked as if there had been no need to bake a cake. Not that there was any *need* to make a cake for Emyr, but after her conversation with Dora she felt the urge to pamper Emyr, to please him and to look after him. She went out for a second time to call the cat and noisily shake the box of biscuits, but there was no sign of her.

And then Emyr was in the kitchen.

'I smelled that from a mile away,' he said, looking at the cake in the middle of the table.

'And I can smell you too.'

'Sorry.'

And Emyr backed out of the door and pulled off his overtrousers and filthy boots. He came back into the kitchen and looked at Anna's leg without its heavy plaster.

'That's an improvement. You'll have to work at strengthening the muscles, though.'

Anna nodded, expecting him to enquire further about her leg, but he didn't; he just went to the sink, washed his hands and sat down at the table.

'That brown cat with the golden eyes – she yours?'

'Have you seen her?'

'She's out there eating a rabbit. That's one helluva cat!'

Anna cut him a generous slice of cake and placed it neatly on a plate in front of him. Emyr ate the cake in silence, and afterwards picked up every crumb by moulding them together with his fingers. He asked Anna about Maria and – as if the cat had heard herself being discussed – she jumped in through the window and walked straight to the kitchen door, mewing insistently to be let through to go upstairs.

'She doesn't usually go upstairs unless I'm going to bed,' said Anna, as if that excused the cat's brazenness.

'You were always soft-hearted when it came to animals. Where did she come from?'

Anna explained that Siôn had brought her, that a friend of his was looking for a home for her and that she, Anna, had been thinking of having another cat, although she hadn't told anyone.

'Odd, isn't it? Strange that he should turn up with a cat, and me wondering about having a cat again?'

'There's a lot of odd things going on.'

But although she sat quietly for a minute or two, he didn't elaborate. Anna started to chat about this and that, but running under her chat like subtitles on a screen were the words 'Dora's right.' I'd better ask, she decided.

'Is everything okay, Emyr?'

'Well ...' As Emyr hesitated, Anna whisked the sugar bowl out of his reach.

'I've heard most of your secrets, Emyr Jones. One more won't make much difference.'

And that was true. For two naturally reserved and private

people, they had entrusted secrets to each other many times. Perhaps because they realised that confidences would not be betrayed. And perhaps because they were sure that neither would wish any harm on the other, and that they would never judge one another.

'No, I'm okay, you know.'

And after he'd gone, Anna tried to remember which words he'd emphasised.

23

FOR HALF A SECOND, MAYBE LESS, SOME HALF-CONSCIOUS, sleepy part of her brain believed it was Ioan's voice she was hearing on the phone. There was a tiny hint in the 'Anna?' And then the voice went on, 'It's Huw here. Ioan's brother. I happen to be in north Wales and thought ... I wasn't sure if you still lived there, but ...'

Very often, there's no time to think about the best decision. To open the door or to close it.

'Would you like to come over, Huw? It would be ...' Anna hesitated for a moment before saying precisely what was on her mind. 'It would be lovely to see you.'

They agreed that Huw would come over in a few days' time, after the conference he was attending was over. Neither one of them was keen to extend their conversation on the phone. All questions could wait until they met. But the moment she'd hung up, Anna regretted that she hadn't asked more, regretted asking him over, regretted she hadn't taken the time to think it over and ring him back.

'He didn't even ask, Maria.' The cat meticulously washed her right paw. 'I offered. Maybe coming over wasn't what he wanted to do.'

Anna tried to remember the short conversation word for word, but failed. Maybe Huw had only intended phoning to say hello. Or maybe he was going to suggest meeting for a coffee somewhere. Anna tried to remember if he'd sounded like someone who had phoned with a purpose, or someone who'd done so on a whim. It was too late now, anyway. She realised she didn't have a number if she wanted to change the arrangement. But why would she want to do that? It would be lovely to see him. Twenty years or more – he'd have aged.

Next to the box of cards in the bedroom where Siôn had slept were the cards Huw had sent Dylan on his birthdays. Three of them, three cards that were too big to fit in the box with the rest. Huw hadn't sent a sympathy card, and he hadn't come to the funeral either. He'd been in America at the time, but there was a letter from him in the box. It was a short letter, genuinely wretched that he would never again see the little boy he'd only met once in his life. Anna remembered how his genuineness, almost selfishness, had been a comfort to her. He wasn't condoling with his brother and Anna, so much as expressing his own grief. But knowing that Dylan was important enough for him to truly regret that he hadn't visited more often had comforted Anna. Anna and Ioan had met Huw in different places after Dylan had died, but he'd never come to Nant yr Aur after the death. He'd come to the flat near the university where Ioan lectured, and he'd joined them for a meal in London, and once in Paris too. But they'd lost touch. Until his call today.

The cat jumped onto her lap.

'D'you know what, Maria? I'm not sure how much I want to know about Ioan. It would be nice to know that he's okay, but I don't want to be prying with Huw. That's not why I invited him here.'

The cat jumped down and started agitating for her supper.

'I'm inviting too many people to this house these days. You're one of them! And you all want bloody feeding!'

She opened the tin of cat food and tried to imagine what tack a conversation with Huw would take. He would ask her what she'd been doing with herself, and how she'd spent the last twenty years. And she'd have to admit to not having done a great deal – just living in Nant yr Aur and scratching a living. Everything else would be in the negative – no, she hadn't had another partner; no, she hadn't had another child; no, she hadn't gone to college, nor travelled much, nor volunteered, nor worked hard and earned a fortune … Huw would be sure to notice that she hadn't made any significant changes to Nant yr Aur – just that the garden had been extended a bit, even though she didn't own the land.

'Use it if you want,' had been Emyr's words to her as he jumped into his Land Rover one day; and a few days later he was back with fenceposts and wire and staples to move his fence.

'Happy birthday,' he'd said as he hammered the last staple home.

'How did you know?' Anna hadn't celebrated her birthday for years, but she got no answer.

Described like that, Anna felt her life sounded sad and pathetic – twenty years and more, and the only thing she had to show for it was a potato patch and an orchard of three trees, and that on borrowed land.

She wondered what Huw had been doing. He had been an architect when Ioan lived at Nant yr Aur. He'd prepared plans for them to extend the house and put in a back door.

'It's silly that you have to come and go through the same door. And building regs will insist you have one, once you ask for planning permission.'

Maybe the plans were still there somewhere, probably with the deeds. But she'd never submitted a planning application. By now, there was no need to extend the house. But many of Huw's designs were bound to be completed buildings by now, and young parents would be walking past them with no memory of how the street had once been. Anna hoped he was pleased with his work – pleased when the dream in his head was realised on paper, and then with bricks, and that he would still be pleased years later when he passed those buildings.

Huw had once sent Dylan a huge box of colourful wooden bricks. After a year or two, Anna had given them to one of Emyr and Dora's lads, and he – according to his mother – built nothing but farm buildings with them. Anna could remember him around their feet in the kitchen of Ty'n Giât, babbling to himself.

'Shed. Big shed.'

Several big sheds had been built in the years following his return from agricultural college. Some people's woodenblock dreams come true.

24

DESPITE STILL BEING ON CRUTCHES, THE FREEDOM OF BEING without the plaster round her leg had given Anna a strange energy. She felt she was getting better. She cleaned and cooked like a maniac, and although it was rather early in the year for proper gardening, there were enough outside jobs to do as well. After a week or so she was depending less and less on the crutches, and was able to do more and more. It was as if the plaster had slowed her mind and her imagination too, but now they were free. She went in search of her passport, and decided to bring the whole box downstairs. It was full of papers considered important when they'd been put there for safekeeping, but there was bound to be a lot of stuff that she didn't need any more. She set the whole lot down in front of the stove, opening its doors so the flames were visible. She sat on the floor, legs extended and ankles crossed. She luxuriated in the fact of being able to do such a thing.

She quickly looked for the passport, and was surprised how close to the top of the pile it was. Inside was a picture of a woman very like her, but younger. She looked at the dates.

'Almost a year left, Maria.'

The cat had sat herself down in a dignified pose between Anna and the warmth of the fire, facing the flames. She didn't turn round, despite Anna addressing her.

'That settles it. I'm going somewhere. For maybe a week, that should be plenty long enough. Who shall we get to look after you, eh?'

Before she could dig further through the mountain of paperwork, the phone rang. She considered staying sitting, but ignoring a phone call is difficult. And maybe it was Huw, wishing to change their plans. But it wasn't Huw. It was Siôn, wanting to know if she was home.

'Yes, I'm home. I'm always home.'

'You weren't home on Wednesday. So I thought I'd make sure today.'

Anna said nothing for a second, just let different feelings move through her mind like sheep leaving a pen, rushing out one after the other, with no idea where they are going.

'I was at the hospital having the plaster off. I'm home now.'

Anna hung up and went back to the box and the fire and the cat. She managed to put a name to the feelings created by one short, simple phone call – guilt was one, but hot on its heels was some ambiguous emotion that made her prickle.

'I don't have to be here, do I, Maria? Maybe for you. But not for anyone else.'

Anna gazed, unseeing, at the papers, trying to understand what was wrong with her. She had always been so pleased to see Siôn. As she'd tried to explain to Emyr, his presence in Nant yr Aur felt right. But today she had wanted peace. And she'd failed to tell him that.

Siôn must not have been far away when he phoned. He was there inside a quarter of an hour, and Anna was still sitting in front of the fire, sorting the papers in the box. The odd thing had already been thrown into the flames, and she had just finished reading old diaries and was deciding on their fate. There wasn't anything important in them, yet their existence and the brief notes in them were proof that she had been doing something. She decided to keep them. She was pulling the deeds from their envelope when Siôn walked in. There had been a time when she could name the former owners of Nant yr Aur in order, and the dates the ownership had changed from one family to the next. But not now. It was the same as the way new lovers can describe every detail of each other's bodies, while couples that have been together for years are sometimes not even completely sure of the colour of each other's eyes.

'Reminiscing, are you?'

'Yes, that's what I'm doing. But that wasn't the plan.'

Siôn came closer to the box.

'Will you make tea for us, Siôn? And I'll clear these out of the way.'

She was sorry she hadn't cleared them straight after his phone call.

'Don't stop just because of me.'

Siôn knelt down beside her, reaching for the papers on the top of the pile and studying them. Anna looked at him reading the deeds of Nant yr Aur.

'Only a few different families have lived here.'

'Yes.'

And that was the end of the discussion. Siôn put the deeds

to one side and looked in the box again. Next were Huw's plans for the extension.

'Wow, were you thinking of altering the old place?'

'At one time. Years ago now. To be honest, I don't know why I've kept the plans.'

And yet she knew full well why she'd kept them. They were there for the same reason that the hardly-used passport was.

'Wow,' said Siôn again, his nose in the plans. 'There'd be another door if you'd done this.'

'True. But there's no need for one.'

Anna pushed the deeds back into their envelope, swept all the papers higgledy-piggledy back into the box and pushed it away. She hadn't even had the chance to look again at Huw's plans but, unlike the list of now-forgotten former Nant yr Aur owners, she could recall every detail of the plans. She and Huw had been the ones who had discussed them; even when Ioan was there, he'd been perfectly content to leave the decision-making to her. For the first time ever, Anna wondered if maybe that was when the distance between them had started. But then again, it wasn't the house itself that had been important to Ioan, but its location. She could almost believe that Ioan would have gone along with things, even if she and Huw had decided on total demolition and building a new house on the site.

But Anna was a nightmare customer for an architect. She'd realised this later, but she also knew she'd be ten times worse if something similar needed doing now. Huw would prepare large scale drawings and post them to her and then explain them over the phone.

'This means knocking a hole through that wall there, you see.'

And a sentence like that would create almost physical pain, the anxiety of someone about to go to the dentist or about to take a much-loved animal to the vet. She knew it was silly, and she never admitted her feelings to anyone; it was easy to conceal her feelings from Huw because their discussions were by phone. Nevertheless, he would try to think of some other way to do things, and each time she would choose whichever design meant the least possible change to the house. But there was no getting around the fact that one of the thick stone walls would have to be breached to extend Nant yr Aur. It would have to be attacked with a pick and sledgehammer.

She and Ioan had been sure that more space was needed. Neither wanted Dylan to be an only child. Or maybe it was she who'd been certain that she didn't want Dylan to be an only child, and Ioan who'd been certain that more space would be needed if they were to have more children *and* Anna was determined to stay at Nant yr Aur. She tried to recall any discussion of this between them, but couldn't. Not that it was important, they had both been of the same opinion.

'Do you have a girlfriend, Siôn?'

'Yes.'

'You've never mentioned her.'

There was silence for a minute.

'You didn't ask.'

'Does she have a name?'

'Siwan,' and he smiled the way everyone does when they speak the name of their lover aloud.

Anna wondered if she should ask him to bring her with him the next time he called. But what if she didn't take to the girl? Or what if she did – that could be worse. For a second she saw a young couple lying in each other's arms down by the river, but she wasn't sure who they were.

'I'll go and make us that cup of tea. You look tired, Anna.'

25

ANNA DIDN'T GET MUCH CHANCE TO TALK TO SIÔN ABOUT Siwan, nor about anything else. Dora came in, with one of her grandsons.

'I'm minding this one at Ty'n Giât. And we both need to get out of the house.' Dora mimed tearing her hair out. 'I'm too old for this!'

Thankful that she could now move with relative ease, Anna quickly shoved the box of papers behind her, and went to the kitchen door.

'Could you make enough for one extra, please, Siôn?'

'Sorry, have you got visitors?' Dora asked.

'Only Siôn.'

Dora looked puzzled. 'Who's Siôn?'

In the gap between Anna realising that she didn't know who Siôn was, and having to decide the best way to explain him to her, the child escaped his grandmother's hold and climbed onto the window sill. By the time he'd been rescued, Siôn had come into the room carrying tea for the three adults and a small mug of juice for the little one.

He bent down to him and in a serious voice asked, 'Can you drink out of a proper cup like this, without spilling your drink on Anna's floor?' The child nodded his head sagely and drank the juice down in one.

'Right,' Siôn said to him, 'how about you and me go for a walk down to the river to see if there's any fish today, and leave these ladies to drink their tea and have a chat.'

As they disappeared through the door, Dora turned to Anna and said, 'Whoever he is, I like him!'

And Anna heard herself saying that she hadn't had the opportunity yet to discover much about his family, but he'd started to call regularly at Nant yr Aur. She explained how comfortable she was in his company from the outset, and the fact that he felt 'right' in Nant yr Aur. She realised that she'd spoken those words before.

'But ...'

'Yes?' said Dora, seeing her hesitate, 'but what?'

'I don't know.'

This was always the danger with Dora. There was something about her, maybe the endless way she chattered on which, once in a blue moon, made one talk without restraint as well. And reveal too much. Dora didn't insist on knowing, but a few times Anna had been aware that she'd said too much to Dora, and then realised that Dora had not reciprocated, despite her non-stop flow of words.

And Dora wasn't one to keep a good story to herself. And neither did she retell a good story without improving on it, if needs be, and even if there was no need. Anna recalled hearing some much-embroidered version, years ago, of the story of her own visit to Hay with that Martin person. She succeeded in tracing the source of the tale back to Dora, but there had been no point saying anything to her. There was no malice in her. It was essentially innocence on her part.

And here she was again, almost charming Anna into saying too much. Anna was on the verge of explaining that, essentially, the problem was that too many people were calling at Nant yr Aur, explaining about Huw's phone call, and saying that he'd be coming over in a couple of days' time. She was grateful that neither the sons nor the daughter-in-law at Ty'n Giât were as nosy as Dora, and that they wouldn't bother telling her if a strange car drove up to Nant yr Aur.

She could imagine Dora going home and telling Emyr about 'this young man that Anna's friends with'. And Emyr quietly listening without bothering to tell her that he'd met Siôn, and that Siôn had contacted Anna in the first place to try and buy Nant yr Aur. It was odd, this belief she had, that Emyr would be faithful to her, willing to keep a secret.

She realised she'd been sitting opposite Dora without saying a word for several minutes.

'I'm sorry. I'm terribly tired today, Dora. Maybe I've been doing too much since the plaster came off.'

Dora left shortly after that and Siôn came back into the house. Anna roused herself into starting a conversation but before she could say a word Siôn had pulled his laptop out of his bag.

'Can I be cheeky, Anna? There's something I need to write and I thought that Nant yr Aur would be the ideal place to do it. Would you mind if I go and work in the little bedroom?'

'Of course not.'

What else could she say? She sat by the fire, with the box that contained her passport and the deeds and the plans behind her, listening to the sound of Siôn's tread as he went upstairs to Dylan's bedroom, and a few of the roof slates secretly shifting.

26

ANNA HAD ABOUT TWO HOURS ON HER OWN IN HER HOUSE between Siôn leaving and Huw arriving. It's true that she'd seen little of Siôn; he had shut himself away in the bedroom and had hardly said a word to her, but he had been there. And then two hours with nobody, during which she opened the windows wide, although it wasn't a warm day, and then closed them one by one, looking at the view from each as she did so. And as she closed the last one she saw a strange car coming up the road, then disappearing for a moment behind a rock and then reappearing.

Anna was out sweeping the step by the time Huw parked his car. She stood at the door watching him walk towards her. Seeing Huw at Nant yr Aur did not make her feel odd. The two brothers were dissimilar in appearance, and Anna was grateful for that. But then he came closer, and greeted her, and that made things more difficult. The voices were similar, and voices age less than bodies. She forced herself to look at him and consciously note every physical detail to counteract the voice.

They stood with their backs to the house for a few minutes.

'Ioan loved this place.'

Well, thought Anna, Huw has decided that they are going to discuss his brother. She paused for a moment before responding. She wished to sound sensible and friendly. And if she managed to sound sensible and friendly, maybe she could conduct herself that way.

'There's nothing stopping him coming here if he wishes to, you know. It's his choice to stay away.' She observed Huw's expression. It was clear something was paining him. 'We never fell out, you know,' she added, hoping to comfort him. 'Just drifted apart. So far apart there was no way to connect ... I'd be happy to see him, I'm pretty sure of that ...'

'Aren't you going to offer me a cup of tea, Anna?'

They went inside and Anna filled the kettle. Neither said a word until they were both seated at the table.

'Anna, did you get a letter from me a few months back – early November?'

'No.'

In the small hours, long after Huw had left, Anna tried to remember the exact words he'd used, but couldn't. She wanted to remember the precise words, to be sure she'd understood properly, to be sure she hadn't imagined things. And yet she longed for it to be something imagined. Huw explained how he'd written to her the day after Ioan had died. How he'd assumed – as she'd neither replied nor attended the funeral – that Anna no longer lived at Nant yr Aur, or that it didn't matter to her. Something along those lines was what he'd said. She knew she'd asked questions and had been answered. Cause of death? Throat cancer. Where had he been living? Nantes in Brittany.

She was able to remember the conversation from then on.

'What made you phone the other day, Huw?'

He explained that he'd heard that she was still living in Nant yr Aur and had suspected that she hadn't received the letter for some reason. He added that he'd felt sure, after only a few seconds on the phone with her, that she wasn't aware of Ioan's death. Because of that, he'd decided not to tell her over the phone.

'But you invited me over, didn't you? I didn't have to ask. I was so pleased you did that.'

And that voice, that bloody voice, so similar to Ioan's, explaining all this. She must have made food for Huw – there were dirty dishes in the sink – they must have talked about other things. She could remember some of the conversation. Huw still worked as an architect. He'd been with his present boyfriend almost nine years. By a strange coincidence, they had Burmese cats – pure-bred pedigrees, half a dozen of them – and he showed great interest in Maria when she appeared from somewhere, although she totally ignored him.

Anna was envious of the cat now, sound asleep beside her on top of the quilt. She felt as if she'd never be able to sleep again. She was compelled to rake up every recollection of Ioan she could from the depths of her memory, and to do it all tonight. But the memories were stubborn – she found it difficult to pull any threads together. All she could remember, all she knew, was that she and Ioan had loved each other and had trusted each other. But tonight she couldn't have proved that coherently to anyone.

'Who do you need to prove it to, Anna?' she said aloud in the emptiness of the bedroom. But she didn't know the answer. She was sure she'd never indulged some hope that Ioan would return to Nant yr Aur, at least not after the first few years. That wasn't what was disturbing her. But tonight she needed to know for certain that those good times *were* good times.

Maybe she should have asked Huw more about Ioan's life, asked what he'd been doing for close on a quarter of a century. But, in all honesty, she didn't want to know. It was enough for her to know that there had been a period – many years – when they had been true to each other, sustained each other, and had considered each other the most beautiful human being in the world.

For the first time in weeks, Anna heard Ioan's voice in Nant yr Aur – or, rather, his laugh – and multicoloured strands of memory came abruptly back to her. She fashioned a quilt from them, and slept.

27

ALL THE FOLLOWING DAY ANNA BROODED. BUT SHE DID NOT reminisce about Ioan. That was something that had been and gone in a flood last night. She played a game of 'what if, what if' all day. What if this had happened, and what if that other thing hadn't ... and the whole thing turned in her head, like a round. Endless variations, but the same basic melody woven through. What if Dylan had lived? And what if she had been willing to leave Nant yr Aur? But he did not. And she could not. Once she had decided on those things, she started on chores around the house, but before long the same two questions would somehow re-surface – through the mop that was touching the floor or the cloth touching a wall at that moment.

Suddenly she'd had enough. She left the mop and the cooling cloudy water in the bucket, dirt sinking to the bottom, and put on her coat and walking boots. She stuffed an apple and a bar of chocolate into her coat pocket and strode out of the door, closing it behind her. Behind Nant yr Aur, not far from the rock that birthed it, a kissing gate opened onto the sheep walk, the ffridd. And from there a path led to the top of the ridge that separated the head of this valley from the next. Anna had not walked the path to the top in years, and she wasn't sure if she could make it all the way up today. She took a stick with her, thinking it would be useful. She had decided two days ago that she would no longer use the crutches.

Maria started to follow her across the coarse grass.

'Shoo! Go home!'

She kicked some loose stones on the path towards the cat. Her golden eyes grew wide in surprise before she turned and walked quietly and haughtily back down the path to the house.

'Sorry!' Anna shouted after her, but Maria did not acknowledge the apology. Anna started climbing the path once more. It was not easy – her leg still felt feeble after the weeks in plaster, and she was short of breath from walking far less lately. She kept going, stopping often to catch her breath. Each time she paused, she would turn to look back. And with every turn Nant yr Aur looked smaller, and it was possible to gain a wider and wider perspective. More farms in the valley to begin with, but after a while she was aware of a new horizon, one that was moving further away from her. After a while she could see the sea, and imagine what was beyond it.

She was starting to really tire by now, and when she saw a flat rock beside the path she sat down on it. She pulled the bar of chocolate out of her pocket, ran her nail along the silver paper and broke off two squares. She put them in her mouth, but rather than chew them, she let them melt with warmth and saliva.

Ioan had gone walking more often than she had. He would walk as if on a route march, and she would be struggling to keep up with him; he would have to wait, sometimes reluctantly, for her to arrive. She had a clear memory of him waiting on this very same rock, and standing up as she arrived.

'Hang on! I need a rest too.'

And him immediately recognising his mistake and smiling, and hugging her, and sitting down once more on the rock and feeding her with chocolate and letting her lean against him. They didn't go any further that day. They just moved a little way from the rock into a hollow that was more or less hidden from view. Before they moved into the hollow Emyr had walked past – a busy man walking swiftly down the path in the course of his day's work. He'd greeted them, and Anna could hear the embarrassment and the touch of jealousy concealed in his laugh.

She had only once been for a walk with Emyr. Their personal space had been long-established inside the solidity of four walls, and as far as the garden or the yard, but when they'd walked together on the ffridd, things had been different. Anna had spent the whole time conscious of the fact that they weren't touching each other, and wondering what exactly her motivation had been in suggesting they go for a walk together. And when they'd returned to Nant yr Aur, and Emyr– in his usual way back then – had put his arm round her and kissed her lightly on the cheek as he left, Anna knew there would never be anything more than that between them. And yet, as she'd realised by now, their friendship deepened after that day. Something had been discussed, but not in words. And a decision had been made. Once in a blue moon Anna wished things could have been different, and today was one of those days.

'You're cowardly, Anna Morris,' she said aloud to the whole valley stretched below her. 'A bloody coward!'

A stonechat rose out of the heather a couple of yards in front of her and flew a short distance before landing again.

'You can't even do that, you stupid woman!'

She put her hand in her pocket and broke off another piece of chocolate before standing up and starting to walk once more. Although Nant yr Aur was now in the distance, the ridge seemed as far away as ever. She felt an unfamiliar, sharp pain in her ankle, and decided that she wouldn't try and reach the ridge today.

'Another time.'

Saying it out loud would maybe make it happen, and she knew, could recall, that the view down the other valley was worth seeing. She was determined to get there, but she needed something else to aim for today. It would be disheartening to turn back at a random spot that could not be named, simply because that was the place where the pain in her ankle became unbearable. She wasn't far from the mountain wall, where the sheep walk ended and the open hill began. There was a cluster of sheepfolds there – she would go as far as that and then head for home.

She reached the sheepfolds and sat down. The folds had been built in a slight dip in the land, sheltered from the wind, and when she was sitting she couldn't see Nant yr Aur. She leaned against the wall of the largest fold. It was perfectly, absolutely, quiet there. She ate her apple and the last piece of chocolate before getting up and starting down the path. As she made her way through the heather she could see Nant yr Aur anew. A car was moving slowly along the valley road towards the sea, but it wasn't a familiar car.

28

IN HER DREAM, ANNA WAS BACK IN THE SHEEPFOLDS NEXT TO the mountain wall. But in place of the peace of that afternoon, they were full of sheep and she was among them. Some of the sheep were flying, white clouds above her head, and the rest were pushing against her and carrying her in the midst of their flow towards the sheep dip. She could smell their wool and their shit and the chemicals of the dip. Maria appeared on the sheepfold wall, mewing and mewing at her.

In the dream Anna shouted at her, 'I'm okay. Go home. I might as well stay here'. But the cat continued to walk round the fold wall, mewing, and she could hear the noise above the bleating of the sheep. Gradually, Anna became aware that she was hearing Maria mewing in real life. Anna surfaced, and the dream dispersed, but the mewing went on and there was an odd smell in the room – something was burning the back of her throat. She began to cough and realised with a jolt what was happening. Nant yr Aur was on fire!

It was only later, looking back at that night, Anna saw that her response had been a strange one. She hadn't been concerned for her welfare, nor that of Maria but, rather, for the house itself. For a split second she had considered staying put and letting whatever would be, be. But Maria was still walking back and forth on the bed yowling and somehow her howling penetrated the madness. Anna grabbed the cat and went past Dylan's bedroom and the open bannisters overlooking the living room. The smell of smoke was stronger there, but she could see that the fire was in the kitchen, and that the door between the kitchen and the living room was closed. A trace of smoke, like the white wool of her dream, was beginning to flow under it.

As they started to go down the stairs, Maria heard the sound of the flames and tried to break free from Anna to go back to the bedroom. Anna held her tightly by the scruff, but not before the cat had drawn blood, clawing at her hand and arm. She reached the door, and succeeded in opening it without losing her grip on the cat. Once outside, she let her go, and saw her flee in fright down towards the river and out of sight. Something strange happened to time. Anna felt she had been standing there for ages watching the cat run away, the house burning away behind her. Then the strange feeling had disappeared, and she was running back indoors and snatching the phone off the oak table.

She phoned, the fire engine came, the flames were doused. Later, when people asked her, she couldn't add anything to the story. She sat on a wall in her nightdress watching the whole commotion, but she couldn't remember the details. One of Emyr and Dora's sons came over, put her in his car and took her down to the village to his parents' house. She drank a cup of tea, and followed Dora to a small, tidy bedroom. She lay down under a flowered duvet and fell asleep.

When she woke up the next morning, for a moment she had no idea where she was. And then she moved over to the small pink washbasin in the corner of the bedroom and started throwing up. The tea to start with, and then endless empty retches.

Dora tried to insist that she eat breakfast, but she could not. She had to content herself with persuading Anna to drink half a cup of tea.

'Would you like me to take you up there now?' asked Emyr.

Anna nodded, got up, thanked Dora for providing her with refuge, lending her clothes, and the tea. The list was endless, but that would do for now. She walked out to the Land Rover. Neither said a word on the way to Nant yr Aur – Anna was in her own world, imagining what they would face, and Emyr was imagining how Anna would react.

Initially, there was less damage than either had feared. The roof and windows were intact.

'Well, at least it's still standing,' said Emyr.

Anna smiled at him. With trepidation they got out of the Land Rover and walked to the door. Anna placed her thumb on the latch and pushed, and the door opened. They were assailed by the strong smell of the smoke, and they stood there without a word. Anna wandered through the house, with Emyr trailing behind her. The kitchen was a complete mess, with the damage from the fire compounded by the water used to extinguish it. But the rest of the house was a surprise – all the walls were black from the smoke, every piece of furniture was disgusting to the touch, but no more than that. Anna was thankful for the stout oak door that led to the kitchen, and for the amazing thickness of the walls, even the interior ones.

Anna started to open every window. She turned to Emyr, smiling. 'It's okay, isn't it. Thank you for bringing me home.'

'You can't stay here, Anna.'

She smiled at him. 'This is where I live, isn't it? There's a roof over my head, isn't there?'

Emyr started to argue with her, and Anna was surprised. She couldn't remember Emyr doing anything except concurring with her, or ignoring her. She interrupted him.

'Don't worry. I'll do all the right things – the insurance, the fire service, all the sensible stuff that needs doing. But I have to be here, there's a lot of work to do. The house needs me.'

Emyr ignored her last sentence. 'Your cat's decided to stay too.'

Maria was walking in through the door. They could almost see her wrinkling her nose in disgust. She went straight to Anna and mewed to be picked up.

'Look at her, the little madam! Look what you did to my arm last night!'

'You should be grateful to her. Without her ...'

Anna suddenly wanted Emyr to go. She wanted to be left alone in the house. And he understood, of course.

'You know where we are. I'll come over tomorrow. You'll have a better idea by then what you intend doing.'

'Thanks, Emyr.' She reached for him and squeezed his hand for a moment, then let it drop just as quickly.

'I'm alright, you know. Look – no plaster on my leg, I've got a car, I've got a phone. And, yes, I know where you are.'

After he'd gone, Anna went to sit on the doorstep with the cat on her lap. She made a mental list of all the things that needed doing. She went back inside, picked up the phone, and worked her way through every last item on the list.

29

THAT FIRST NIGHT AFTER THE FIRE WAS BOTH HORRENDOUS and magnificent for Anna. She worked extraordinarily hard all day and managed to make part of her bedroom fit to sleep in. It still reeked of smoke, but she had clean bedclothes, thanks to the launderette in town. She could have asked Dora if she could use her washing machine, or begged a favour at Ty'n Giât, but she didn't want to speak to anyone. She fell into the sleep of the dead, but was certain that she would be able to get the house into shape reasonably soon.

By the time Emyr arrived the next morning she was in tears.

'Right, are you ready to change your mind and come and stay with Dora and me?'

'This is where I want to be. You know that, Emyr.' She wiped away her tears, which created black smears across her cheeks. 'I just suddenly realised how much work there is to do.'

Emyr looked at her in silence for a while. 'Have you contacted the insurance company and so on?' he eventually asked.

Anna nodded. She didn't want to acknowledge that those tedious things had to be done. Part of her believed, if she stayed long enough in Nant yr Aur, that the damage would undo itself, like a wound mending. She would wake one morning to see the kitchen curtains complete and back in their place, and by the end of the next day the crockery, which had been smashed to smithereens when the shelf fell, would be back on the shelf, whole and clean, and in about a week there'd be nothing to show for the fire except a dark strip of scarring high up on the wall.

But she also knew that wasn't going to happen. She knew she'd have to share Nant yr Aur for weeks with noisy workmen listening to a bilingual commercial radio station. Yesterday, she'd had to force herself to make the phone calls that would start the process – the same way she'd forced herself to go back to the hospital with Dylan when she saw the symptoms returning. Maybe it would have been better to have ignored them and remained at home, and maybe better for her to live forever in the small portion of the house she'd managed to clean, live there eating cheese sandwiches for lack of a kitchen.

'Yes, Emyr. There's someone coming over this afternoon. Fortunately, the phone still works.'

She did take Dylan to hospital, and she did face the tests and the treatments, and the pair of them were imprisoned indoors when he could have been throwing stones in the river. But Ioan had been her rock then, hadn't he? Even when he wasn't there in the flesh, his phone calls and regular postcards were a comfort, reassuring her that she was never alone. She wondered if he'd had to support someone else through a horrific experience. She regretted not having questioned Huw more closely to get a picture of the shape of the rest of Ioan's life.

The insurance company's representative arrived shortly after Emyr left, and started the process by which, in a few days' time, three men arrived at Nant yr Aur every morning at eight. A skip was installed outside and the remains of the kitchen units and other bits and pieces were piled up in it. Anna did not venture into the kitchen to try and salvage anything from the black mess. The hope of retrieving something whole was not enough to assuage the pain of seeing the things that had been ruined. She let them clear everything. But, like someone who cannot leave off picking at a scab, she found herself sometimes drawn to the skip. There she saw her red coffee pot, minus its spout. One of the men passed her with another load.

'This is in one piece, if you want it, missus.'

And he placed the circle of stained glass, covered in soot, in Anna's hand. For a moment Anna almost threw the circle into the skip. She knew, had she not happened to be standing on that spot as the load passed, that it would have gone in the skip – and maybe that would have been for the best. She thanked the lad, the youngest of the three, and ran her finger over the glass, creating a pathway in the soot. She walked down to the river, knelt, and washed it in the cold water, watching the blackness flow away from it.

The workmen had been at Nant yr Aur for a few days before they realised that Anna was still living there. Not that she'd lied, but she hadn't mentioned it until one of them asked over coffee one morning.

'Where are you staying?'

And she admitted that she was camping here without a kitchen or hot water. When the gang left that afternoon, the oldest – the boss – turned to her. 'We're going to work Saturday and Sunday this week – we'll get finished sooner then,' he said.

Sometimes kindness comes from the most unexpected quarters, thought Anna.

She wondered about contacting Siôn, and thought better of it. She didn't want him to see Nant yr Aur like this, so maimed. And if Siôn were to come, he would stay; and after having the house full of other people all day she longed for the hands of the clock to arrive at five. Then, she would hear the sound of their scruffy Transit van drive away, leaving no one at Nant yr Aur except Maria and her.

Emyr called by, of course. And as the workmen got to know her better they started to refer to him as 'your fancy man'. After a while she gave up correcting them and accepted the title and the teasing. When Siôn turned up, like a moth to a flame, she pre-empted them by introducing him as 'Siôn – my toy boy!'

'I'll explain in a minute,' she said hurriedly to Siôn, to the accompaniment of the men's laughter. But Siôn was only half-listening as he stared open-mouthed at the aftermath of the fire.

'What happened?'

'The place caught fire one night. Or, rather, the kitchen did ... an electrical fault, apparently.' She looked at Siôn's concerned face. 'It's coming along, you know. It's improving every day. We'll be okay.'

They went to sit outside. Since the fire Anna had taken to sitting outside more often, and although by now the living room at least was reasonably comfortable, she kept up the habit.

'Why didn't you get in touch, Anna?'

'There was no point. The work's getting done. Emyr calls by. And besides ...'

Anna let the sentence trail off in the middle. Siôn waited a moment before prompting her to continue.

'And besides what?'

'I didn't want you to see Nant yr Aur in this state, and worse, in the first few days.'

'I could have helped.'

'Spring's on its way,' said Anna, changing the subject. She was looking at a crocus pushing its way through the soil about a foot away from them.

They chatted for a couple of hours, but Anna had the feeling she'd given offence by not contacting Siôn to let him know about the fire. Strange how this young man, without any connection to the house, had taken to Nant yr Aur and had somehow found his place there. But then she remembered about a little girl and her dog sharing a cheese sandwich on the doorstep half a century ago, in another world. She could remember the place quietly caressing her. God only knows what nightmares Siôn was fleeing from, although his conversation was almost always cheerful. But if avoiding talk of his problems was part of that escape, what right had she to insist on dragging the real world into the hours he spent at Nant yr Aur?

Thinking about it, she didn't open up to him either. He knew she'd lost a child, and he knew that her relationship with the child's father had ended. But she had presented them as bare facts, things that had happened and were over and done with. It was better that way. It was enough for her that Emyr knew how close she had been to failing to come to terms with that reality. But the fact that Emyr knew almost everything about her had never bothered her.

30

SIÔN INSISTED ON TAKING ANNA OUT FOR A MEAL THAT NIGHT. The work on the kitchen was almost finished, but the cooker had yet to be fitted.

'Come on, no arguments. I've got a car for once, so you don't even have to drive.'

But she had never been one for arguing. She never had any intention of arguing. That was one of the things that attracted her to Ioan. The only time she could remember Ioan raising his voice was when she'd gone out to weed beetroot in the middle of the night. The concept of a man and a woman living together without rowing was so new to her that she'd marvelled at it every day. She knew, from seeing other families and her friends' experiences, that the thing was possible, but to live in a place where no one raised their voice was like an extension of the comfort she got from Nant yr Aur itself. She couldn't imagine one without the other. The relationship between her and Ioan had ended without so much as a curse. Sometimes she suspected that was the reason there was no other man in her life – she couldn't risk bringing someone to Nant yr Aur who might shout at her and defile it.

'Do you row with your girlfriend sometimes, Siôn?'

'No. Never.' He almost looked as if he were ashamed of his answer. 'I've got friends who think it's odd,' he added.

'Maybe they're jealous, you know. And sometimes people don't believe it's possible.'

Anna remembered a young, more fiery Dora telling how she had once thrown all Emyr's clean shirts – and this in the middle of her ironing them and him needing them to go to some farming union conference – into the middle of the cow shit in the farmyard; to finish the job, she had jumped into the tractor and driven backwards and forwards over them. The thing that had enraged her further was that Emyr, after shouting at her to stop, had gone to sit on the farmyard wall and laugh at her, laugh until he rocked with laughter she said.

Anna told Siôn this story as they travelled towards the sea, looking for somewhere serving food midweek. The first two pubs were closed, but there were half a dozen cars parked outside the third, and signs singing the praises of the food.

'Will this do?'

'Siôn, love, I haven't had a meal in a pub for years, and precious few hot meals at all in the last few weeks. I've been without a kitchen for quite a long time, remember. Believe you me, I shan't complain!'

Siôn led her to a small table near the fire and went to the bar to fetch drinks and menus. Anna observed the other people in the pub – one or two couples, a family obviously celebrating some occasion and two men at the bar with the demeanour of nightly customers.

Siôn returned with a gin for Anna and orange juice for himself, and sat down opposite her. The menu was discussed, decisions made, food ordered. After the first course was placed in front of them, Anna said nothing for a while, she just ate eagerly. But then she slowed down and the conversation started up again. Anna had forgotten how chatting in a public space is often different from a conversation at home. Not so much that other people are listening – everyone else seemed wrapped up in their own little worlds – but because every speaker was away from the familiar. She felt that the restaurant operated as a kind of neutral space and, because of this, the conversation between her and Siôn followed a different tack.

'It would be nice to meet your sister and your girlfriend sometime. Bring them over to Nant yr Aur. When the weather is warmer, maybe ...'

Siôn put his knife and fork down on the table and took a mouthful of juice. He picked up the knife and put it down once more, this time on the plate.

'I plan to. But I have something to tell you first. Two things, actually.'

Anna sensed that she needed to listen to him carefully. For a second, no, less than that, she was disinclined to do so. She was enjoying her prawns and her gin and the warmth of the fire, and some inconsequential light chat would have suited her mood. But that was just a flash of stubbornness. She made all her body language tell him that she was listening closely.

'I'm going to be a father in July.'

This wasn't a heartfelt confession to destroy the atmosphere of the meal. She raised her glass and congratulated

Siôn, enquired about the details but, all the same, she knew that the news of a baby on the way was the sugaring of a pill.

She made herself ask, 'And the second thing is …?'

'Huw called to see you?'

'Yes. Ioan, Dylan's father, has died, he came to tell …'

And then she stopped mid-sentence. Something wasn't right. She tried taking a sip of gin, but there was nothing left in the glass except the sharp lemon and melting ice cubes.

'How did you know Huw had been? And how do you know about Huw?'

And Siôn began to explain, releasing fragments of information but without laying them out in chronological order or in order of importance, or in any order as far as Anna could make out. Her role was to sit opposite him, in a pub whose name she didn't know, catching these fragments and rearranging them on the table in front of her to see the picture revealed there.

Huw was Siôn's uncle. Siôn remembered being cross at his father because he wouldn't turn back to retrieve his blue ball beside the beans. His dad had recently died. He hadn't seen much of his dad when he was a small child. His little sister's mother wasn't his mother. He'd been born within a few months of Dylan's death.

More facts were thrown her way, small pieces of multi-coloured sharp glass, and she had no choice but to create a mosaic out of them.

His mother died when he was three years old. At that time his dad became a permanent part of his life, the dad that read him stories and had a kickabout with him.

'That's enough, Siôn. I think I need another gin.'

Anna pulled the lemon out of the glass and pushed the mixture of ice and water towards him. 'Maybe a double.'

She couldn't look at Siôn as he walked to the bar. She didn't need to look – she knew exactly how he walked, she knew exactly the shape of his feet. She chewed the lemon slice in her hand without tasting its sourness; she stripped off every last piece of flesh with her teeth, leaving the rind clean. Siôn returned and placed a large gin in front of her and a small rum next to his own plate. They both drank without a word.

'I think I'm ready to go home now, Siôn.'

Siôn chatted in the car on the way back to Nant yr Aur, but Anna found it hard to concentrate on what he was saying. He managed to get over to her how, following the death of his father, he'd felt a strange urge to return to the place he'd spent his holiday years ago. He couldn't explain it. He'd had several other holidays, but this was the one he remembered.

'And Dad would tell me stories about a little boy called Dylan who used to live here ages ago. He didn't explain then that Dylan was his son, and I'm not even sure if I believed that Dylan was a real boy. And I remember him explaining how the house had grown from the rock behind it long, long ago.'

Siôn stopped the car by the gate. He didn't even kill the engine.

'I'll leave you be for tonight.'

Anna forced herself to say good night to him, but the moment the car disappeared round the bend she regretted that she hadn't held him tight.

31

THE WORKMEN WERE THERE EARLY THE FOLLOWING MORNING with the new cooker.

'Here we are, missus – all that's left is fitting this, bit of tidying, then we'll leave you in peace.'

While they were doing that she went to fetch the circle of stained glass. She threaded a new piece of string through the loop and re-hung it in the window. The morning sun shone through the sunset once more.

By midday everything was done. The men packed all their gear into their Transit van for the last time, and Anna was on her own in Nant yr Aur. There was no sign, even, of Maria.

As they were leaving, the oldest of the workmen looked down the valley and saw the blue Land Rover coming up.

'Your fancy man's on his way. You can make food for him today.'

Anna didn't reply.

'Are you okay?'

Anna invented a headache, and then realised she did, indeed, have a headache. She had slept right through, but felt she had been dreaming all night. The dreams were snippets of classic films, and she was directing, but the actors refused to follow her directions. In one film Ioan was saying that he loved her, and she was trying to insist that he tell the truth.

'But that's what's in the script, Anna. I have to stick to the script.'

She tried to remember if she had any painkillers in the house, yet suspected they would have no effect. She watched the Transit leaving and the Land Rover drawing nearer. She hoped it would turn for Ty'n Giât and that Emyr would be busy for the rest of the day helping and hindering his sons. But Emyr came up to Nant yr Aur, and Anna had no wish to discuss the previous evening with anyone. If she didn't discuss it, she could pretend it hadn't happened. She prayed for one night without the information, as she'd prayed for one more innocent night playing with a small blue car a long time ago.

Emyr took one look at her. 'What's the matter with you?' he asked sharply.

'Come and see the finished kitchen.' She pointed at the glass circle throwing its colours across the floor. 'That's the only thing that was rescued from the fire.'

And Emyr, fully aware of its significance, smiled at her. But the smile she returned was empty. Anna knew she'd have to tell Emyr about the night before. There would be no need to tell anyone else, and she needn't ever speak to Siôn again – there would be no need to do anything with the mosaic and its sharp, unfinished edges. But it was vital that she tell Emyr. If she did not, the information would be like a tiny, tiny crack between them which would grow into a chasm full of dirty water. She made tea, looking in surprise at the new teapot and the new mugs. She had bought them, and had enjoyed doing so. She had spent an entire day spending her money. She had chosen a few things that were similar to those that had been lost, but she had mostly chosen different things. But now, for a moment, she looked at the green teapot and the white mugs as if she had no idea where they'd come from.

'I went out for a meal with Siôn last night.'

She might as well start there. And yet, maybe it would have been better had she chosen a different sentence, one that didn't include his name, maybe; one that didn't include anyone's name. Her story was as fragmentary and chaotic as Siôn's had been, but this didn't seem to make much difference to Emyr. He listened carefully as the tea in front of him grew cold.

'I used to know the story of my life, Emyr. Yesterday afternoon I did know the story of my life. But now I don't.'

'What difference does it make?'

Anna realised that it was extremely difficult to describe the difference between this morning and yesterday afternoon. She'd had a kaleidoscope as a child. One small adjustment and the whole pattern would change completely, change to one with no connection to the previous one. The mirrors inside would multiply any small change and alter every part of the multicoloured circle. She tried explaining this to Emyr. He usually understood her odd, metaphorical explanations. But today he was silent and looked totally lost. He more or less reiterated his first question.

'Would it make any difference if someone had told you? Would things have been better if you'd known about Siôn for years?'

'I don't know. And who could have told me?'

'Me. I could have told you.'

Of course the mugs were new and the teapot was new and the cooker was new and the paint on the clean walls was new. They had to be that way. Because everything had changed. She wasn't even sure if the walls of Nant yr Aur were still in exactly the same place. She was staring so hard at the new crockery on the table she didn't hear the start of Emyr's explanation. And explanation it was, she noted, not an apology. He had made a decision, he said, twenty-five years back, not to say a word to Anna. His conscience had been clear on this until Siôn appeared. Anna heard him explain how he had almost failed to post the letter in case that Siôn Williams was the same Siôn who as a ten-year-old had kicked a ball with him in the garden of Nant yr Aur.

'But I knew who he was the minute I clapped eyes on him. Didn't you see the resemblance to Ioan?'

Anna thought about the question, but was unable to answer. She stood up and collected the mugs, threw the cold tea down the sink, emptied the leaves into the compost bucket, washed the mugs, dried them, and hung them on the new hooks. She was surprised the hooks could take their weight, surprised the walls could take the hooks.

She was aware that she was absolutely starving; there was some emptiness inside her, and although she doubted whether even a shearing-feast would fill that emptiness, she started peeling onions. She sliced them thinly and began frying them, as does everyone when they start cooking but don't know what they're preparing. She moved the onions about in the pan with a wooden spoon, and their smell somewhat counteracted the strangeness of the place.

'Go home, Emyr. Maybe Dora's made food for you.'

32

FOR THE FIRST TIME EVER, IOAN AND EMYR MELTED INTO ONE in Anna's head and then separated again just as quickly. An image came to her of the pair of them. Dylan was sick, but well enough to be allowed out in the garden to play a little, and the two of them, younger men, with a bottle of beer each, out in the sun watching him. That would have been about two months before Dylan died. She hadn't remembered Ioan like that, and she hadn't seen Emyr like that either. But today, that was the only image she had of them. She didn't know who the man was who had held her hand from the moment they'd left the house to the minute they'd stepped back across the threshold on the day they'd buried their son. And the other was no one except a stupid old man who used to live in Ty'n Giât.

Anna couldn't think what to do with the onions. She continued to fry them, watching them start to turn black. Eventually, all she did was to cut two untidy slices of bread, spread them thickly with butter, and put the onions on top with a touch of cheese and black pepper. Even that was almost too complicated. Maria came in and jumped on the table, sensing, as cats do, that today she wouldn't be scolded.

'Just be grateful you're nothing to do with any of them, Maria.'

And as she said it, she recalled Huw explaining how he and his partner bred Burmese cats. Of course, someone who raised show cats wouldn't want to keep kittens that were the result of some stray tomcat getting hold of one of his queens. Anna put her finger in the butter of her sandwich and held it for Maria to lick.

'Don't worry. I shan't ask. I don't want to know.'

She went to sit in front of the fire in the living room. She would have liked to go and sit outside, but it was drizzling and fog was gathering round Nant yr Aur. She wouldn't see anything outside and the damp cold would penetrate through all her clothes; it was the sort of rain that, with practically no force, could find its way through any coat and, eventually, chill the marrow. She put another log on the fire and gave thanks for it and for the four walls around her.

She sat in the chair, her legs folded beneath her. She sat there until she was stiff. She stretched her legs out straight, pins and needles stabbing; she put more wood on the fire and went back to sit in the chair. There was no point in doing anything else. Anna couldn't think what she should do, what needed doing. She tried to imagine what she'd have been doing today if ... She was finding it difficult finishing the sentence. Describing exactly what had changed was difficult.

The phone rang, but she didn't get up to answer it. The postman pushed letters through the door; she left them on the mat. She didn't want more information of any sort. Part of her was surprised that she hadn't asked Siôn for more detail, and surprised she hadn't insisted on an explanation from Emyr. But she knew neither would tell her the truth, only their versions of the truth, like light bent through a prism.

Maybe she should create a slant truth, create a story which would explain why Siôn was conceived, and why Ioan had left without an explanation – without saying he had a son who needed him, a healthy son, a living son. Maybe she could create a story some day, but not today.

She heard a racket behind her, and for one insane moment thought the stones of the house walls were going back into the rock, that they, too, were leaving her, betraying her. But it was only Maria, inside the cardboard box in which Anna kept the deeds of the house. Despite all the clearing and repairs that had been going on, she hadn't taken it back upstairs. She hadn't finished sorting it, and she intended finishing it one day, to get it in order.

The cat leapt out of the box with a mouse squeaking and writhing in her mouth. She dropped the mouse, which ran a few inches before it was caught and then dropped again. The mouse ran and hid behind the coal bucket; Maria waited for a minute, watching it, and then using one paw skilfully hooked it out of its hiding place. The mouse froze in fear or pain and was lightly smacked with a paw to start it running once more. Anna watched all this without feeling anything. She got up from her chair and walked past this theatre of pain as if nothing whatsoever was happening. She took hold of the box of papers and placed it on the edge of the table.

Huw's plans – as well as being dirty from the soot – were covered in mouse droppings and had been thoroughly gnawed into holes. There was no point in keeping them. She went through to the back, to the kitchen where everything was new and unfamiliar, to fetch the compost bucket. She began ripping the pages into strips and dropping them on top of the onion skin. The paper, like the skin, would rot and then nurture.

Under the plans, the deeds were in rather better shape. The fact that they were in an envelope had protected them from the worst damage. She wiped them as best she could and went to fetch a clean, white envelope for them. She put her passport to one side without looking at it, and then continued working her way through the rest of the paperwork. Things that were once relevant were now redundant. There was no point in keeping them.

She became aware of a crunching sound beside her feet. Maria had given up playing with the mouse. She was eating the tiny body delicately, leaving the guts behind; Anna picked them up and dropped them into the compost bucket.

33

TWO OR THREE DAYS PASSED. THE PASSPORT WAS STILL ON THE table, and Anna could have sworn it was growing, that it was a couple of millimetres longer and a couple of millimetres wider every time she looked at it. It would be so easy to put a few things in a bag and drive down the track. For the first time in her life she didn't feel secure in Nant yr Aur.

No one called by and Anna ignored the phone every time it rang. And yet she yearned to talk to Emyr. Not the Emyr who had left the house three days ago, but the Emyr who had existed for the thirty years before that. She wanted to talk with the man who had for so long been her friend, but he had disappeared. He disappeared when he'd said the words 'Me. I could have told you.' That sentence had not rearranged the pattern in the kaleidoscope, it had smashed it completely.

She wondered if Emyr had considered telling her, on occasion, during the decades of conversation about everything else under the sun? Had he been conscious of the thing every time he'd been in her company? Or had he more or less forgotten, had filed information about Siôn in some dusty, far shelf of his brain? Maybe he'd stuffed it there the moment he first knew. Once again, in her mind's eye she saw two men sitting drinking beer in the sun, and this time their faces take on a serious air as they talk. But now they are the faces of two strangers.

And she would have to wait for Siôn to come over before she could face the new past created for her, the past that he was part of. Maybe it was him phoning, but she wasn't about to speak on the phone. She'd have to see him in Nant yr Aur before she could know how much had changed between them. But she took comfort from one thing – she felt no anger at all towards Siôn himself. He had been a child at the time.

Anna was standing in the kitchen when she heard the door opening. For a moment she felt sick. Clearly one of them would call by sooner or later, but she didn't want to speak to anyone today. Tomorrow, maybe.

'It's only me!'

She heard the sound of Dora's shoes click-clacking across the slate floor of the living room. For the first time in her life, Anna felt relief that it was Dora. She entered the kitchen looking like a miniature dragon. Anna could almost see a curl of smoke slide out of her nostrils.

'He's told me! I was right, wasn't I, that something was wrong, that something was bothering him.'

The torrent of words from Dora was worse than usual. For a minute or two Anna thought she was angry with Emyr for not having shared the secret with his wife, but pretty soon realised that Dora was furious with him for what he'd done, and that she sympathised with Anna. She was almost ashamed of her husband.

'Why didn't he understand that what goes around comes around? He knew what was going on, and you in the hospital with the little lad. And Ioan came and stayed here, you know, with that Siôn. I went to my sister's for a while that summer, I never saw him, but ...'

Anna poured tea into the white mugs and put a slice of lemon in her mug.

'And now he's sitting in the house, hangdog, saying he's too scared or ashamed or something to come and see you.'

Anna felt her hackles rising. 'Emyr asked you to come here, Dora?'

'Goodness me, no. He has no idea I'm here.'

Dora paused for a minute, and Anna could almost hear her trying to think of the right words. Then she suddenly continued, more quietly – a toy, a stuffed toy dragon.

'If he does come up here, will you hear him out, Anna? You're important to him. You always have been, and I've always known that.'

Anna must have given some sort of answer, but afterwards she couldn't remember exactly what she'd said. Something along the lines of feeling that everything was falling apart around her, maybe; some cliché like that.

She expected Emyr to come over within days, but he didn't. Instead, early one morning, Siôn arrived. He stood in the door, unsure of his welcome.

'You weren't answering the phone.'

Anna looked at him and considered Emyr's question: 'Didn't you see the resemblance to Ioan?' But she couldn't answer that question now, either. In any case, it wasn't physical appearance that was important. That wasn't why he'd found his place at Nant yr Aur. And yet it was perfectly obvious. He could not be anyone else's son. He was Ioan's son and ... But she couldn't, not even privately to herself, name the other relationship which wove them together. Naming it would be to acknowledge its existence. She touched her hand lightly to his cheek for a moment.

'Are you okay?'

'Yes. Do you want to talk about Dad?'

Anna winced and put her hand on the latch. 'No. Not now.'

They stood at the door for a while, with Maria threading between their legs.

'But I do want to know more about this child that's on the way.'

Siôn smiled, the smile of a happy toddler.

'Siwan's in the car.'

The three of them sat round the oak table drinking tea from the new mugs. Anna moved the paperwork lying there to one side, sliding her passport safely into the back pocket of her jeans. It was in that pocket for a week or more while the presence of the two young people in the house altered her daily routine. Siôn and Siwan completed tasks that had needed doing for a while – she washed all the windows and he injected a chemical to kill the woodworm that had started to attack one of the beams.

***

Anna gazed at the shadows of young leaves moving backwards and forwards across the floor as the breeze rocked the branch. There had been no shadows there yesterday, and soon enough the branches would be bare once more. But today there were leaves and their shadows. She knew that Emyr would arrive at Nant yr Aur sooner or later. She was sure of that, despite becoming a stranger to her overnight. She sipped her coffee slowly while considering this. She watched all the people walking past the small circular tables on the pavement, and imagined the blue Land Rover making its way up the track and Siwan opening the door and walking out to meet him.

'Looking for Anna, are you? She's not here.'

Possibly he'd smile at her. Or maybe not, maybe he'd just look at her belly, which was starting to swell under her tight pink T-shirt, before turning back to his Land Rover without a word. Reversing, ready to drive back to the village or up to Ty'n Giât, he would turn his head and glance at the kitchen window. It would be no more than a rectangle of clear glass. The circle of stained glass would have disappeared, and Emyr would know that Anna had gone.

SIAN NORTHEY HAS BEEN A FULL-TIME WRITER FOR THE LAST fourteen years. Almost all her work is written and published in Welsh. She is the author of three novels for adults, one poetry collection, three short story collections, several scripts, and numerous children's and teens' novels. Her novels are *Yn y Tŷ Hwn* (Gwasg Gomer, 2011), *Rhyd y Gro* (Gwasg Gomer, 2016), and *Perthyn* (Gwasg Gomer, 2019). In 2022 she co-edited the bilingual poetry anthology *A470:Poems for the Road/Cerddi'r Ffordd* (Arachne Press, 2022).

Sian Northey is also a literary translator. She translated into Welsh the memoir *The Journey is Home* by John Sam Jones, and Alys Conran's debut novel, *Pigeon*, which in its original English won the Wales Book of the Year Award in 2017. Both books were published in English and Welsh by Parthian Books in 2021 and 2016, respectively. She recently translated the award-winning *The Last Firefox* by Lee Newbery (Penguin Random House, 2022) under the title *Y Llwynog Tân Olaf* (Firefly Press, 2022).

SUSAN WALTON HAS BEEN COMMISSIONED TO TRANSLATE books from Welsh to English for the publishing house Gwasg Carreg Gwalch since 2009. She has had fourteen translated books published, including eight novels for older children/young adults. During 2020 Susan was mentored under the Literature Wales scheme as an emerging literary translator.

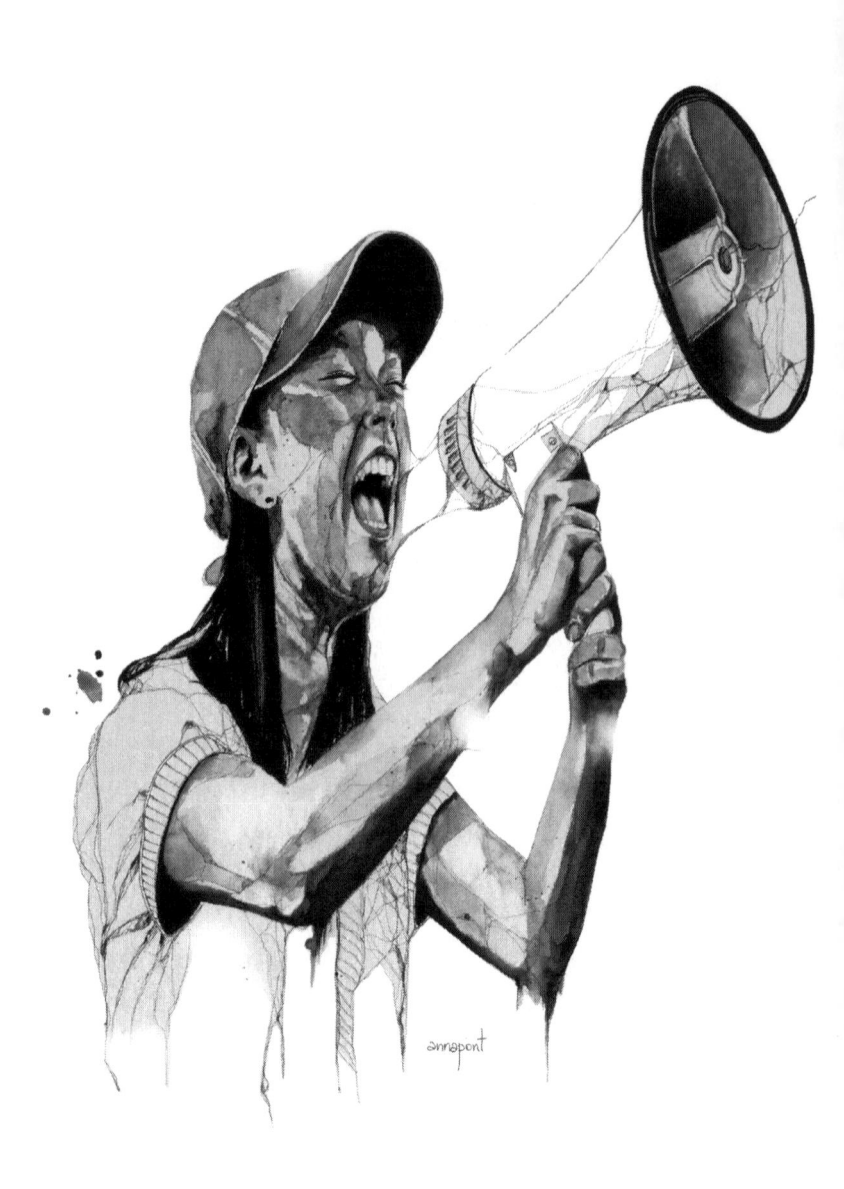
annapont

We translate female authors who write in minority languages. Only women. Only minority languages. This is our choice.

We know that we only win if we all win, that's why we are proud to be fair trade publishers. And we are committed to supporting organisations in the UK that help women to live freely and with dignity.

We are 3TimesRebel.